NEW YEAR AT MISTLETOE LODGE

A Feel-Good Christmas Romance

A Novel by

AMY RAFFERTY

VIP READERS

Subscribe Here!

Don't miss the
Giveaways, competitions,
and 'off the press' news!

Don't want to miss out on my giveaways, competitions and 'off
the press' news?
Subscribe to my email list.
It is FREE!
Go to https://dl.bookfunnel.com/daorxdf4jo

FOLLOW ME ON MY SOCIALS HERE

Not only can you check out the latest news and deals there, you can also get an email alert each time I release my next book.
Follow me on Bookbub
https://www.bookbub.com/profile/amy-rafferty

I always love to hear from you and get your feedback. Email me at-
books@amyraffertyauthor.com

Follow on Amazon-
https://amazon.com/author/amyrafferty

Sign up for my newsletter and get a free gift,
https://dl.bookfunnel.com/et26h8ozl3!

Join my 'Amy's Friends' group on Facebook
https://www.facebook.com/groups/1257329798446888/!

OTHER BOOKS BY AMY RAFFERTY

THE BAKERY IN BAR HARBOR - *Secrets in Maine Series*

CUPIDS BOW RANCH - *Montana Country Inn Romance Series*

STARTING OVER IN NANTUCKET - *Cody Bay Inn Series*

LEAVE A ROSE IN THE SAND - *Starting Over in Key West Series*

A MYSTERY AT SUMMER LODGE - *A Coastal Vineyard Series*

CHARMING BOOKSHOP MYSTERIES - *Small Town Beach Romance*

MOONLIGHT DREAMS - *Honey Bay Cafe Series*

NANTUCKET CHRISTMAS ESCAPE - *Second Chance Holiday Romance*

RETREAT - *Manatee Bay Series*

SECRETS OF WHITE SANDS COVE - *A San Diego Sunset Series*

THE SEA BREEZE COTTAGE - *La Jolla Cover Series*

THE MCCAID SISTERS - *The McCaid Sisters Standalone*

CHRISTMAS AT MISTLETOE LODGE - *Feel Good Christmas Romance*

BOX SETS

NANTUCKET CHRISTMAS ESCAPE BOOKS 1-3 - *Second Chance Holiday Romance*

A MYSTERY AT SUMMER LODGE: Complete Collection - *A Coastal Vineyard Series*

SECRETS OF WHITE SANDS COVE: Complete Collection - *A San Diego Sunset Series*

THE SEA BREEZE COTTAGE: Complete Collection - ***La Jolla Cover Series***

CODY BAY INN: Complete Collection - ***Nantucket Romance***

STARTING OVER IN KEY WEST: Complete Collection - ***A Flordia Keys Romance***

MONTANA COUNTRY INN: Complete Collection - ***Montana Country Inn Romance Series***

MANATEE BAY: Complete Collection - ***Treasure Seeker Beach Romance***

CHARMING BOOKSHOP MYSTERIES: Complete Collection - ***Small Town Beach Romance***

HONEY BAY CAFE: Complete Collection - ***Second Chance Beach Mystery***

Three in One

COASTAL COLLECTION: Sea Breeze Cottage, Mystery At Summer Lodge, Secrets At White Sands Cove - ***Three Series In One Book***

Spanish Versions

El Café de Bahía Honey - ***Honey Bay Cafe (Spanish)***

Escapada Navideña a Nantucket - ***Nantucket Christmas (Spanish)***

Bahía de Manatee - ***Manatee Bay (Spanish)***

La Posada de la Bahía Cody - ***Cody Bay Inn (Spanish)***

INTRODUCTION TO NEW YEAR AT MISTLETOE LODGE

Set against the enchanting backdrop of Mistletoe Lodge, Frisco, Colorado, this heartwarming novel captures the essence of the holiday spirit and the joy of finding love when least expected.

New Year at Mistletoe Lodge is a heartwarming romantic novel that follows the intertwined lives of Heather and Giles as they navigate the complexities of love, their destiny, and second chances.

Set against the backdrop of a charming lodge nestled in the Tenmile Mountain Range during the holiday season, the story beautifully captures the essence of this magical time of year and the transformative power of love.

Heather Jessop is back at Mistletoe Lodge for the festive season. She is the hyperactive Wildlife Veterinary explorer to her family, forever seeking her next adventure. What her family doesn't know is the real reason Heather is home. She was severely injured on her last assignment and has been forced to take sick leave for three months while she heals. There's no better place to recover than with family during the festive season at Mistletoe Lodge in Frisco, Colorado. Heather hasn't been back there for two years after a fight with her cousins, and it is time to patch things up. Heather knows things were bad at the lodge, but she hadn't realized just how bad until she meets the lodge's new investor, the handsome and charming Giles Holland.

Giles Holland is looking for a new challenge. He managed to build an empire from scratch, with branches in many different industries, including real estate. When his good friend Avery Hawthorne offers him a chance to invest in a lodge in Colorado, it piques his interest. Giles has been after Avery for years to head up a new business venture to help save the smaller corporations from being swallowed by the larger ones.

Thrilled at the prospect of Avery finally considering his offer and eager to check out his new investment, Giles heads for Frisco, where he finds his greatest challenge yet: Winning the heart of the free-spirited Heather.

THE RESIDENTS OF NEW YEAR AT MISTLETOE LODGE

MAIN CHARACTERS:

Heather Jessop
Giles Holland

OTHER CHARACTERS:

Priscilla (Venter) Carlisle - Heather's grandmother
Emily (Carlisle) Saunders - Heather's cousin
Hank Saunders - Emily's husband
Baby Saunders - Emily and Hank's baby (not born yet)
Ryder Carlisle - Heather's cousin (and the male lead character in Book 1)
Avery (Hawthorne) Carlisle - Ryder's wife and Emily's best friend
Rosie Carlisle - Ryder's daughter
Mary Holland - Gile's mother
Patrick Holland - Gile's father

(Additional Characters Have Not been Listed)

PETS & ANIMALS:

Rory - Two-year-old golden retriever (Rosie Carlisle's dog)
Saviour - Five-month-old jaguar
(Heather rescued the baby cub from a poacher's snare)
Jasper - Bald Eagle
(He has lived at Mistletoe Lodge for 18 years.
Heather found him with a broken wing when she was ten, and
he was 11 months old)

CHAPTER ONE

eather Jessop moved stealthily in the heart of the Amazon rainforest, where the verdant canopy stretched endlessly overhead. Her senses heightened to the symphony of life surrounding her. The dense undergrowth beneath her boots whispered with every step she took, each rustle and chirp telling a story of creatures hidden from view. She was on a mission, guided by her unwavering dedication to preserving wildlife.

It was early July, the heart of the wet season, and the jungle was alive with a vibrant energy. Drenched by the unrelenting tropical rains, Heather's khaki-clad form was a splash of earthy color against the lush, green backdrop. Her golden ginger hair was tucked under a practical safari hat. At the same time, a knapsack filled with medical supplies rested on her back, and a small medical cage swayed in her hand.

The call had come in earlier in the day. A local tribe had reported a baby jaguar caught in a poacher's snare. Without hesitation, Heather had embarked on a solo rescue mission. Her heart pounded with anticipation and concern as she navigated through the tangled flora and vines, guided by the tribe's descriptions.

Sweat glistened on her brow as she pushed forward. Heather had always been at home in the wild, and her life's mission had led her to confront situations most would deem dangerous. But in the face of danger, she stood resolute.

"Come on, Heather," she whispered to herself. "You've got this."

The sounds of the jungle enveloped her—the distant cries of howler monkeys, the rhythmic hum of cicadas, and the occasional ripple of water from a hidden stream. She knew she was drawing closer to her destination.

As she pushed through a particularly dense thicket, Heather spotted the faint glimmer of sunlight reflecting off the jagged metal wire of the snare. Her heart ached at the sight. She had to act quickly. Every moment counted.

She approached with caution, her trained eyes assessing the situation. The baby jaguar—a small, spotted ball of fur—was trapped, its panicked eyes filled with terror. The jaguar's mother had likely abandoned it, unable to free her cub from the cruel trap.

"Hey there, little one," Heather murmured, her voice soothing. She reached for a tranquilizer dart in her bag, slowly loading it into her tranquilizer gun. Heather knew she had only one chance to make this count. She steadied her aim, breathed in deeply, and squeezed the trigger.

The dart found its mark, and the tiny jaguar slumped to the ground, its frantic struggles ceasing. Heather rushed to its side, her heart heavy with worry and relief. The snare was still caught around the cub's leg, and she carefully began to untangle the metal wire, her hands trembling with urgency.

Heather couldn't help but marvel at the jaguar's beauty as she worked. Its fur was a tapestry of intricate spots and rosettes, a testament to nature's artistry. This creature deserved a chance to roam the wild, to grow into the magnificent predator it was meant to be.

Finally, the jaguar's leg was free from the snare, and Heather wasted no time administering first aid. She checked the cub's vital signs, cleaned and dressed the wound, and carefully monitored its condition. She stood and radioed her team for a rendezvous, her voice filled with triumph and concern.

"Team, I've got the cub. We need an extraction ASAP. Meet me at the designated coordinates."

Heather felt a sudden, sharp pain in her leg as she spoke. Startled, she glanced down to find the baby jaguar had woken from the tranquilizer, and in its disoriented state, it had lashed out with its claws, deeply embedding themselves in her calf.

Heather gritted her teeth against the searing pain and continued her call, fully aware of the situation's urgency. The extraction team promptly acknowledged her request, assuring her they were en route. Heather managed to sedate the cub again and secured it inside the cage she'd brought.

Realizing the importance of stopping the flow of blood streaming from her leg and ensuring her safety from potential predators, she swiftly wrapped a makeshift bandage around her wounded calf. With the jaguar safely secured, Heather returned to her rendezvous point. The relentless rain drenched her clothes, but her determination propelled her forward. Her leg throbbed with fiery pain, and she was starting to realize that her injury was more severe than she had initially thought.

Time seemed to stretch endlessly as Heather navigated the rainforest, her senses attuned to every sound and movement.

The cub, now calmer, slumbered in the cage she held against her, finding solace in her presence. In moments like this, Heather deeply connected with the wild creatures she dedicated her life to protecting. It made all the risks and pain worthwhile.

Finally, the welcome sound of the extraction team's approaching helicopter echoed through the trees. Heather's heart soared with relief, and she signaled their location with a flare. The helicopter descended, and the team swiftly took charge of the injured jaguar and their fearless leader.

Heather was lifted to safety, her leg still throbbing. As the helicopter rose into the sky, the rainforest fell away beneath her. She couldn't shake the feeling of a deep connection forged in that jungle. Her heart sank with the realization that it would be some time before she could continue her mission to save the jaguars due to her injury.

The helicopter's blades sliced through the humid air, carrying Heather and the rescued jaguar away from the dense Amazon rainforest. The roar of the engine was deafening, but Heather hardly noticed. Her focus was on the small, wounded cub nestled in its cage. Despite her pain, she couldn't help but feel a deep sense of satisfaction in saving this young jaguar's life.

The journey back to civilization felt like an eternity. Rain pounded against the chopper's windows, its relentless rhythm a backdrop to the anxious whirring of the helicopter's blades. Heather clutched her injured leg, willing herself to stay conscious. She knew her survival was crucial to the cub's chances of a full recovery.

After what felt like hours, the helicopter touched down in a clearing near a small village on the outskirts of the rainforest. The local rescue team was waiting, their faces etched with relief as they saw the injured jaguar. Heather carefully handed the cub over to their capable hands, her fingers trembling from pain and exhaustion.

"Take good care of him. I've called him Savior," she told them, her voice weak but resolute. "And make sure he's released back into the wild when he's ready."

The team nodded in understanding. With the cub safely in their care, the rescue team wasted no time preparing Heather for her evacuation. Her leg ached mercilessly, and the telltale signs of infection were already setting in. She was carefully loaded onto a stretcher and transported by ambulance to a nearby medical facility, the bumpy ride causing every jolt of pain to shoot through her body.

The clinic, a modest building in the heart of the village, was basic but well-equipped. Heather's face was drawn as she was wheeled inside, her vision blurring from a mix of pain and exhaustion. Though lacking in resources, the local medical staff were skilled and dedicated. They immediately began assessing her injury and treating the jagged wound on her calf.

Over several days, Heather's fever raged. Her days blurred into a haze of sweat-soaked nightmares and fits of delirium as the medical team battled to control the infection in her leg. She was lost in fevered dreams of the jungle, jaguars, and her determination to protect the wild.

In her moments of lucidity, she would glance out the small window of her hospital room. The village starkly contrasted with the lush jungle she had left behind. Simple huts were scattered along the muddy streets, and the villagers went about their daily routines with a sense of calm foreign to Heather's fast-paced world.

One evening, as the sun cast a warm glow over the village, a young girl from the village approached her bedside. The girl's eyes were curious, and she carried a bouquet of vibrant tropical flowers.

"For you," she said with a shy smile, offering the flowers to Heather. "You saved the baby jaguar."

Heather managed a weak smile in return and accepted the gift. The act of kindness from a stranger in this remote corner of the world warmed her heart. It reminded her of the inherent beauty amid adversity and renewed her determination to heal. That memory was the last of the memories of the village as Heather's fever once again spiked.

The medical capability of the small village clinic proved insufficient to provide Heather with the specialized care her deteriorating condition required. With the infection rapidly spreading and her leg deteriorating at an alarming pace, Heather's life hung in the balance. She was urgently airlifted by air ambulance to Los Angeles, a journey she barely remembered as she waned in and out of consciousness.

Upon her arrival in Los Angeles, she was rushed to St. Mark's Hospital, a renowned medical center known for its expertise in complex cases. The infection had taken a severe toll on her leg, necessitating multiple surgeries to remove the affected tissue and repair the damage to save her leg from amputation.

Weeks turned into slow, arduous months of recovery. The infection had been successfully treated, and Heather's leg began to heal, but the journey ahead was long. It would be some time before she could return to work in the jungle or walk properly. After several months of rehabilitation and two additional surgeries to address complications caused by the prolonged infection, Heather was finally released from the hospital.

However, she faced another challenge, as her mobility was still far from perfect. She would require ongoing physical therapy to regain her strength and ensure her leg's full functionality. In addition, her doctors strongly recommended that she take it easy and allow her body time to heal fully. The toll of the months-long ordeal had left her physically and emotionally drained.

By the beginning of December, her injuries had healed to a point where she could walk without too much pain, and the doctors were confident she'd need no more operations. She was at a point where if she never saw another hospital again in her life, it would be too soon.

Her first stop after her latest doctor's visit was to see her boss at the Los Angeles offices of Wildlife Vets International.

Heather was eager to get back to the jungle and her quest to save the jaguars. She knocked on Nancy Dulling's office door and entered when her boss's cheerful voice invited her to.

"Hi, Nancy," Heather greeted the well-groomed and dressed director of the Los Angeles branch of the organization. Nancy was a retired wildlife vet who had been forced into retirement after an incident with a bison nearly ended her life.

"Hello, Heather," Nancy greeted her with a warm smile, her brown eyes assessing Heather. "How are you?"

"I'm all healed and ready to return to the jungle." Heather sat in the chair Nancy waved to.

"I applaud your eagerness to get back to the jaguars," Nancy told her, pushing her designer glasses onto her head as she leaned back in her plush office chair. "But, sweetie, I've received the letter from your doctor, and they have not signed you fit for duty yet." She handed Heather the letter. "They recommend at least three more months of recuperation."

"The operative word being recommended," Heather pointed out, handing the document back to Nancy. "I feel fine and eager to get back to work."

"How's the pain?" Nancy asked her.

"Gone," Heather lied, a twinge of guilt surging through her. "My only pain now is in my heart for the animals I should be helping but can't."

"Nice try," Nancy said with a knowing smile. "But I noticed your slight wince as you sat down and knocked your leg on the desk."

"That was because I knocked my leg," Heather defended her actions and grinned. "I think everyone would wince if they hit a part of their body on a desk." She knocked the oak top. "Especially as this is old solid oak."

Nancy tilted her head and stared at Heather for a few seconds in contemplative silence before sighing and shaking her head. "I'm sorry, Heather." Her eyes filled with worry. "You're our best vet and team leader, and while it pains me to do this, I have to go by the doctor's recommendations." She gave Heather an encouraging smile. "I know you're eager to get out there. But chancing it now may lead you to give up going out in the field altogether." Her brow furrowed. "Don't forget I've been where you are now, and I went back into the field too soon and against doctor's orders." She opened her arms, gesturing to her office. "Now I'm desk-bound."

"But your injuries had you near death's door," Heather pointed out. "Mine was just my leg that is now healed."

"Oh, sweetie," Nancy sighed. "Your injury was just as severe and had you near death, too. You just don't remember it. I was at the hospital when you were brought back to Los Angeles."

"Okay!" Heather gave up the fight, knowing she was not

going to win. "Fine. But can we revisit this in a month instead of three?" Her brow knitted together pleadingly. "I'm going to go insane if I don't get back out in the field soon."

"Fine, it's a deal," Nancy agreed to Heather's terms. "But we let the doctors decide."

"Agreed," Heather said with a nod and blew out a breath. "I just wish it wasn't over the festive season."

"When did you last spend Christmas or New Year with your family?" Nancy asked her.

"I'm not sure," Heather shrugged. "Three, maybe four years ago."

"Then it's high time you did," Nancy told her. "As your boss, I'm ordering you to relax and have a family festive season this year and see the new one in with them, too."

"That's a bit impossible as my grandmother is in Frisco, Colorado, for Christmas," Heather explained. "And I'm not supposed to squish onto an airplane for three to four months."

"Well, it's lucky for you that we have a few helicopters at our disposal," Nancy reminded her. "Let me know when you'd like to go to Colorado, and I'll organize it for you."

"Seriously?" Heather shook her head, trying to look pained about the thought of having to fly to Colorado for Christmas, but the idea was more appealing than she let on.

"Yup," Nancy nodded. "Pack your bags and get ready to head to Colorado."

It was eleven days to Christmas when Heather found herself in one of the organization's jets, making her way to Denver. Once there, she was met by one of the organization's helicopter pilots who was going to fly her to her family's cherished lodge nestled on the outskirts of Frisco. The anticipation swirled within her as she gazed out the window, her eyes drinking in the snow-covered landscape below. The mountainous terrain, cloaked in a blanket of pristine snow, unfolded in all its majestic splendor.

The helicopter's descent marked her first return to Mistletoe Lodge in four years. While Heather spoke to her grandmother at least twice a week when she could, she'd not told her grandmother about her injury. Heather had also not spoken to her cousins, Ryder or Emily, since she'd voted to sell the lodge a year ago. The whirring of the blades against the crisp mountain air filled her ears, a comforting and familiar sound. Her heart danced with the prospect of reuniting with her family and relishing in the holiday season she had missed in recent years.

With a soft thud, the helicopter gently landed, and the scenery before her seemed straight out of a winter postcard. The snow-laden trees sparkled in the winter sunlight, and the lodge, which held many cherished memories, stood resolute against the elements. Heather pushed the door open once the pilot, Wally, gave her the go-ahead. She thanked him, hopped out, and leaned in to retrieve her backpack and Stetson.

With a friendly wave to the pilot, Heather closed the door behind her, her gloved hand twisting the handle before she released it. The helicopter's engines roared to life again, and Heather stepped out of harm's way. With a powerful surge, it lifted off the ground, ascending back into the sky with a sense of graceful power.

The helicopter incited a swirling mist of snow that wrapped around Heather. She plopped her Stetson on her head and watched the aircraft rise into the sky, flying off in the direction it had come. She sighed and turned to scan the scene before her. Heather was delighted and surprised to see her cousins standing watching her from the other side of the driveway that separated them.

Her face lit up with a warm smile, and she waved at them before shouldering her backpack filled with the essentials she would need for her vacation and headed toward them. Heather forced herself not to limp as the cold gripped her injured leg, making it feel like an icy hand dug its long nails into her calf.

"Hello, hello!" Heather beamed, her cheeks pink from the chilly air. Dropping her pack carelessly in the snow, she bounced into her cousin Ryder's arms, kissing his cheek. "Hey, Ry, it's good to see you."

Not waiting for his greeting, Heather greeted his sister, Emily.

"Emmy!" Heather wrapped her arms around Emily. As small as she was, she lifted Emily off her feet as she squeezed, once again ignoring the slicing pain the exertion caused her leg. "I've missed you soooo much."

"Hey, Heather," Emily greeted her.

"Rosie?" Heather dumped Emily back onto her feet and turned to Rosie, Ryder's nine-year-old daughter, who took a step behind Ryder. "My word!" She observed Rosie. "How you've grown in two years."

"Hi," Rosie said shyly, cowering behind Ryder.

Heather turned her attention to Hank, whose eyes narrowed at her warningly, but that didn't deter Heather. She gave him a cheeky grin and went in for a hug.

"You're still making grand entrances, I see, Heather," Ryder said as Heather unfolded herself from hugging Hank.

"Gran always says a lady must make an entrance to be noticed." Heather laughed, saying, "I heard the festival was back on, so I thought I'd come to lend a hand."

"Aren't you supposed to be counting polar bears in the Arctic?" Emily asked.

"Tagging," Heather corrected her. "Tagging polar bears."

"You were tagging polar bears?" Rosie's curiosity outweighed her shyness as she looked at Heather and stepped away from her father.

"I did," Heather confirmed. "Do you want to see some pictures?" She pulled her phone from her bomber jacket pocket to show a fascinated Rosie.

"Oh, wow!" Rosie's eyes were huge. "Look, Daddy." She pointed to a picture of Heather sitting beside a polar bear that had been tranquilized.

"Yeah, Heather does a lot of dangerous stuff like that," Ryder said as if in warning, making Heather frown at him.

"I want to go work with polar bears, too," Rosie told him.

Heather's frown turned into a smile as she looked at the beautiful child, remembering how she, too, had been fascinated by wild animals at Rosie's age.

"Heather doesn't only work with polar bears, sweetheart," Ryder explained. "She's a wildlife vet, which means she works with all sorts of wild animals."

"That's so cool," Rosie said, staring at Heather in awe, and Heather's smile broadened.

"If you're trying to scare her away from being like Heather," Hank laughed, patting Ryder's shoulder. "You're not doing a good job of it."

"What's wrong with being like me?" Heather asked.

She pocketed her phone and picked up her well-worn backpack, glancing at Ryder questioningly and feeling hurt by his cutting remark.

"Nothing," Emily assured her, rolling her eyes at Ryder. "Just Ryder being a protective father."

"Ah!" Heather nodded and moved the conversation away from her work. Her family didn't know that her arctic trip had been over two years ago. "So, how's the preparation going?" She looked curiously at Ryder and Emily.

"Thanks to the weather, we've only just been able to get started," Emily told her.

"So that means you could use an extra hand around here?" Heather grinned at Ryder.

"You're always welcome at the lodge, Heather," Ryder said through gritted teeth, his shoulders tensing up, making Heather realize he was still angry with her. "This is your home too."

"Are you still mad at me for voting to sell this old place?" Heather tried to make light of their argument over a year ago.

"For the purpose of keeping the peace for the festive season, I'm going to ignore what you just said," Ryder informed her stiffly. "We're done here for the day."

"Come on, Heather, let's get you settled." Emily linked her arm through Heather's. "I'm sure Grandmother's going to be thrilled to see you. You're going to have to stay in her cottage with her as we're filled to capacity."

"Not a problem," Heather said, glancing at Ryder before they started walking toward the lodge and smiling at Emily. "It will be like the good old days."

"Daddy, can I go with them?" Rosie asked, stopping Emily and Heather as they waited for his reply, and he nodded.

Rosie's excited call summoned Rory, the golden retriever, and he bounded toward the trio before they continued their walk. As Heather walked, the crisp winter air kissed her cheeks, and her senses drank in the serene beauty of the landscape. The earthy scent of snow underfoot and the distant sounds of animals in the fields combined to create a feeling of peace.

When they rounded the bend, the lodge emerged from the surrounding woods, revealing its rustic charm and welcoming facade. Heather's heart swelled with a profound sense of belonging and nostalgia. The lodge was more than just a building; it was a repository of her family's history, love, and traditions. The towering pines and snow-draped eaves seemed to embrace her like old friends.

Once they crossed the threshold, the lodge's interior embraced them with its warm, cozy atmosphere. Heather was met with the delighted surprise of her grandmother, Priscilla Carlisle, and the lodge's chef, Nora Preston. Their warm smiles and welcoming presence tugged at Heather's heartstrings. The bonds she shared with her family were unbreakable, transcending the years and miles that had kept her away. With its rustic beauty and loving family, the lodge had a magical way of melting away the worries and hardships of the outside world.

At that moment, the fierce passion for preserving wildlife that had always driven her took a back seat. It was her calling, her purpose, but for now, it was on hold, allowing her spirit to embrace the tranquility of the holidays and focus on healing. The lodge was the perfect place for that, a sanctuary where time seemed to slow, and every creak of the wooden floor whispered tales of cherished moments.

CHAPTER TWO

T en days before Christmas, Giles Holland was far from looking forward to the impending festive season. His parents were on a cruise, leaving him to his own devices. The painful memory of his engagement to Kinsley Bamford ending a year ago, after he had caught her cheating on him, still lingered. That experience had left him hesitant about dating again, particularly in a world where people seemed more attracted to his wealth and status than his character.

Giles had worked hard for his success. He wasn't the product of a trust fund or a silver spoon upbringing. His parents were humble. His father was a dedicated Fire Chief, and his mother ran a small bakery. He cherished his parents deeply, loving them more than any material possessions.

Apart from his family, Giles held another person dear to his heart: his best friend, Avery Hawthorne. Avery had chosen to spend the festive season in Frisco, celebrating with her loved ones. Meanwhile, Giles found himself bombarded with invitations to numerous Christmas functions, typical for someone of his stature. Yet, he rarely attended these events, prioritizing privacy and only joining those that were absolutely essential. For him, Christmas was a time to be with family and friends, not to mingle with strangers.

As he contemplated the prospect of escaping to a secluded resort, an email from Avery suddenly popped up in his inbox. Intrigued, Giles clicked on it and began to read. Avery's message was about Mistletoe Lodge, which belonged to her friends, the Carlisle family. The name struck a chord in his memory.

Ryder Carlisle, who had once broken Avery's heart, was part owner of the lodge along with his sister, Emily. Giles squinted, recalling the intricate web of emotions that had entangled his best friend.

As he read Avery's passionate plea for help, explaining that she was trying to save Mistletoe Lodge from being bought up by a large resort chain, Giles felt a spark of curiosity and a newfound interest in the lodge's fate. He decided that maybe, just maybe, this would be the perfect escape he needed from the suffocating expectations of the holiday season.

Giles meticulously scanned the projects mentioned in Avery's email, his intrigue growing with each line. Saving small businesses from being consumed by larger corporations was more than just a professional endeavor for him; it was a personal mission born from his family's painful history.

As a child, he had seen his parents lose everything when they were cheated out of their family-owned bakery in a middle-class Los Angeles neighborhood. His mother's exceptional baking made their little bakery a local treasure. However, their livelihood was abruptly taken away when a colossal corporation embarked on a property acquisition spree. The family was left with nothing, and they had to downsize to a small one-bedroom apartment with a tiny loft that became Giles's bedroom.

Giles smiled as he thought of his parents. His mother had become an influential figure on the board of one of his companies, where she dedicated herself to assisting small mom-and-pop stores just like the one they had lost years ago. Her passion and expertise played a significant role in providing opportunities for others to preserve their businesses.

On the other hand, his father continued to serve as an honorable firefighter and climbed the ranks to become the Fire Chief. He still held firm to his humble beginnings and values, which had served as a foundation for Giles's commitment to helping others.

Giles reached for the intercom button.

"Hi," Barb Gardner, his assistant, answered.

"Barb, I need you to find out all you can about Frisco, Colorado, and Mistletoe Lodge," he asked her.

"Sure," Barb said. "Anything in particular you're looking for?"

"Just the usual." Giles rubbed his upper lip thoughtfully. "I'm thinking of investing in the area."

"No problem. Give me a couple of hours," Barb said.

Giles grew curious about this place and its significance to Avery, particularly her dedication to preserving it.

Over the years, Giles and Avery had collaborated on numerous projects, fostering a close professional relationship. He had initial concerns when she joined Grimes Mergers and Acquisitions, fearing that the corporate environment might harden her and diminish her compassion. To his delight, Avery's heart seemed to expand even further while working for that company, her empathy unwavering.

Despite Giles's repeated attempts to entice her, he had been unable to persuade her to leave Grimes and head up a property investment company for him. Avery's loyalty and commitment to the causes she believed in remained unwavering. Now, as he delved into the details of Mistletoe Lodge, he couldn't help but wonder how this new project might lead her down a path she hadn't anticipated.

Giles stood and turned toward the ceiling-to-floor windows that offered a panoramic view of the Los Angeles shoreline. The glimmering sea stretched out beneath the sunlight, evoking thoughts of snow-capped mountains in his mind. A smile slowly curled his lips as he decided to opt for a traditional snowy Christmas in Colorado this winter, appreciating the change from the usual resort destinations.

His thoughts then turned to Avery's impending meeting with Ryder, her ex-fiancé, who had left her at the altar twelve years ago. It had always puzzled Giles how someone could commit such an act, especially considering Avery's remarkable qualities. He recalled their first meeting at UCLA, where he had initially harbored a significant crush on her. Yet, as their friendship deepened, he knew he would never jeopardize their special bond. Avery was not only one-of-a-kind but also the most loyal and protective friend one could hope for.

Giles nonchalantly shoved his hands into his pockets as he stared past the ocean, his mind engrossed in a nascent idea. It felt somewhat nefarious, but he believed he might have discovered a way to extricate Avery from the corporate machinations that never truly valued her at Grimes Mergers and Acquisitions. According to Avery's email, the company had manipulated her into persuading the Carlisle family to relinquish their lodge, using the enticing promise of a promotion she rightfully deserved years ago.

A surge of anger coursed through him. Grimes was attempting to squeeze the compassion out of Avery by making her betray her friends. Despite the heartbreak Ryder had caused Avery years ago, she would never compromise her loyalty to the Carlisles, especially since she still regarded Emily Carlisle as one of her closest friends. Giles shook his head, wishing Avery had reached out to him before rushing to Colorado. They could have collaborated to find a solution. He detected the unspoken truth in her email, understanding that Avery was striving to save the lodge before revealing her true intentions to the Carlisles.

Giles was distracted from his thoughts when his office door swung open, and he heard Barb's angry voice.

"You can't go in there!" Barb hissed.

His hair stood on end as a female voice said haughtily, "I'll go in *whenever* I please."

Giles's fists clenched at his side, and he took a deep breath before turning to see Kinsley flounce into his office in front of an angry Barb.

"I'm sorry, Giles," Barb apologized, her eyes blazing as she glared at the well-dressed and groomed blond woman whose lips formed a sultry smile as their eyes met.

"It's okay, Barb," Giles reassured her.

"You have an appointment in fifteen minutes," Barb reminded him before reluctantly leaving the office and closing the door behind her.

"Hello, darling," Kinsley purred, walking toward his desk.

"What are you doing here, Kinsley?" Giles asked with a raised eyebrow, not moving from where he stood.

"I was wondering if you were invited to Ashley Forsyth's ball this year?" Kinsley batted her perfect eyelashes.

"You know I'm always invited to Ashley's Christmas Ball," Giles said, his eyes narrowing suspiciously as he had a hunch where this conversation was going.

"Are you going?" Kinsley's lips split into a smile, and her eyes turned a smoky blue.

"Ashley's ball is for a good cause. I will be going as usual," Giles answered. "What do you want, Kingsley?"

"To go with you to the ball," Kinsley's smile broadened prettily.

"I already have a date," Giles lied. "I'm taking Barb."

"Your *assistant?*" Kinsley spluttered in disgust. "Ashley's ball is the event of the year." She stressed. "Everyone who is someone will be there. You can't take a..." She huffed, searching for a word. "An assistant. She's a single mother who's never been married and will probably wear something off the rack."

"What's wrong with off the rack?" Giles crossed his arms and looked at her in disgust. "You do know that Ashley makes off-the-rack clothing?" A smile lifted the one side of his mouth. "I'm sure she'd be delighted to see a guest wearing one of her creations instead of the overpriced clothing she abhors."

"I..." Kinsley's eyes turned stormy as she looked at Giles, appalled. "Is this your way of getting back at me for a little slip-up?"

"A little slip-up?" Giles laughed. "If going away for a weekend with Stanley Burke is a slip-up, I'd hate to see what your major mistake would be."

"So, you are still mad at me." Kinsley pouted.

"No, Kinsley. I'm not mad at you," Giles corrected her. "I always suspected what kind of person you were. You just drove it home for me." He looked at his wristwatch. "If there's nothing else, I must prepare for my next meeting."

"Giles, you can't take your assistant to the ball of the year!" Kinsley ignored his hint for her to leave. "You'll regret it."

"Why don't you get Stanley to take you?" Giles suggested, pulling back his chair and slipping into it.

"Because..." Kinsley stopped, pursing her lips.

"He wasn't invited?" Giles looked up at her with raised brows.

"I'm sure he was," Kinsley said. "But he's not going."

Giles knew she was lying as Ashley had already told Giles she'd not invited them as she couldn't stand either Stanley, the biggest playboy in California if not America, or Kinsley. Kinsley was the spoiled princess of developer James Bamford from Bamford Development.

Ashley, Giles, and Avery had met at UCLA and became fast friends. Ashley was the heiress to Forsyth Investments. She'd started her own affordable clothes, cosmetics, and perfume company without her father's help. Ashely had turned her small business into a multi-million dollar one. Ashley had married a racing car driver, Brand Frampton, who they had also met at UCLA.

"That's a shame." Giles looked pointedly at his wristwatch once again. As annoyed as he was getting with her, years of good manners instilled in him stopped him from kicking her out. "I'm sorry, Kinsley, but I have to get back to work."

"I don't care!" Kinsley hissed, leaning on his desk and looking him angrily in the eyes. "You can't take a little nobody to Ashley's ball. It's my reputation on the line as well." Her cheeks started to redden with anger. "I can't have people think you left me for *her*."

"Barb. *Her* name is Barb," Giles reminded her. "And people already know we broke up over a year ago when you returned from your trip with Stanley."

"Why can't you just get over that?" Kinsley pushed herself up and folded her arms. "You know Stan and I grew up together and have a past."

"We all have a past Kinsley." Giles sighed, shaking his head.

He was so tired of having this argument with her, which he'd had nearly three times a month since they'd split. She kept calling or dropping in on him to get back together.

"Exactly!" Kinsley gestured with her hand. "You were poor once, and I don't hold that against you."

Giles's anger started to burn inside him, and its flames slowly consumed his good manners. "Kinsley, I think you need to leave," he said through gritted teeth.

"No, I'm not finished here," Kinsley refused. "Not until you tell your *help* that you're taking me and not *her* to the ball," she said stubbornly.

A knock distracted him, and Barb popped her head through the door. "Giles, your appointment is here."

"Give me a minute," Giles told her before turning his attention back to Kinsley, and he pushed himself to his feet. Enough was enough. "I think you should leave before I call security."

"Excuse me?" Kinsley stared at him in shocked disbelief. "You can't throw me out."

"I can, and I will!" Giles warned her. "I've put up with you looking down your spoiled nose at others and your snide-cutting remarks while we were together. To be honest, you going off with Stanley was the best thing that could've happened to our relationship."

"What?" Kinsley gasped, her eyes widening. "You can't talk to me like that."

"I think someone needed to a long time ago." Giles knew he was being nasty and rude, but he'd had enough of her self-possessed outlook. "Now, please leave before I force you to do so. I have someone waiting for me."

"My father is going to hear about this!" Kinsley's voice was laced with venom. "And you know what happens to people who anger him."

"Trust me, Kinsley, your father will do nothing about it." Giles raised his eyebrows warningly.

"Yes, he will." Kinsley sneered. "He'll ruin you."

"Please leave, Kinsley." Giles clamped his jaw, his eyes narrowing dangerously.

Kinsley stormed out of the office and nearly knocked over Barb, who Giles hadn't noticed was still standing at his office door.

"Wow!" Barb exclaimed, gaping after Kinsley before turning to Giles. "Does she realize you own more than half of it after you bailed out her father's company two years ago?"

"It's not for me to tell her." Giles shrugged, pinching the bridge of his nose and shaking his head, feeling rattled. Kinsley had a way of irritating him that took irritation to another level. "Please give me two minutes before sending my appointment in."

"Sure." Barb nodded, looking at him worriedly. "Are you okay?"

"I'm getting a splitting headache." Giles gave her a tight smile. "Oh. What are you doing tomorrow night?"

"Curling up in front of the television to watch kiddy movies with Oscar," Barb answered.

"If I get a babysitter for Oscar and buy you whatever you need, would you accompany me to Ashley Forsyth's Christmas Ball?"

"What?" Barb gasped. "You know I hate those things."

"I know, but I kind of told Kinsley I was taking you." Giles grinned at her pleadingly. "Please don't make a liar out of me."

"It's such short notice." Barb racked her mind for excuses. "I would need to go to a salon to have my nails done."

"You can have the day tomorrow. Go to a spa. Find the top place, and I'll get you in and pay for it." Giles told her.

Barb's eyes narrowed. "A spa day, grooming, and a new outfit?"

"Yes." Giles nodded. "And we'll close the company four days early for the festive season."

"All this just to go to the ball with you?" Barb looked at him.

"Yes." Giles nodded again. "And I'll owe you a favor."

"A huge favor." Barb pointed out. "Fine."

"Great." Giles breathed a sigh of relief.

"You know, I'm sure you could've gotten any of the gorgeous single socialites in Los Angeles to go with you," Barb told him. "And it wouldn't cost you as much as this is going to."

"It will be well worth every penny," Giles assured her, fishing out his credit card and handing it to her. "There you go."

"Wow, I get the black card!" Barb walked to his desk and took the card. "But this will also cost you a dinner for Oscar and me tonight."

"Deal." Giles laughed. "Go nuts."

"Never say go nuts to a woman with an unlimited credit card." Barb gave him a smug smile as she walked out of his office. "I'll send Mr. Arnold in."

"Thank you." Giles waited for his next appointment.

Five days later, Giles was preparing to make arrangements to go to Frisco when his office phone buzzed.

"Giles, I have Priscilla Venter from Venter and Associates on the line for you," Barb told him. "Do you want me to put her through or take a message?"

Giles frowned. His first thought was that, even though Ashley's mother had sent Kinsley a late invitation to the Forsyth's ball, she was making good on her threat. Not that it phased him. Giles just didn't have the time for any of Kinsley's malicious plots, but he couldn't avoid the call either. Everyone took calls from Priscilla Venter, the controlling partner of the renowned Venter and Associates.

"Sure, put her through." Giles sighed, pinched the bridge of his nose, and spoke as soon as the call was put through. "Giles Holland."

"Good day, Mr. Holland." Priscilla's calm voice drifted through the phone.

He knew better than to be taken in by it. Priscilla didn't get her reputation as one of America's top attorneys by being a soft pushover. Giles had seen her in action and had often made a note never to find himself at the other end of a legal battle with her. If he was a gambling man, she was also someone you wouldn't want to play poker with. She had no tells. Opposing counsel never knew when she was going in for the kill.

"Hello, Ms. Venter," Giles said politely. "How can I help you?"

He gritted his teeth, waiting for Kinsley's bogus claim, and tried not to let it annoy him by picturing snow-capped mountains.

"I believe Avery Hawthorne has put a proposal together for

you to invest in Mistletoe Lodge," Priscilla surprised him by saying.

Giles's surprise turned into a frown, and he opened the folder with all the details Barb had gathered for him on Mistletoe Lodge, scanning the page for their legal representation. His eyes widened when he saw it was right there but listed as Ms. P. Carlisle, and it suddenly dawned on him why he'd missed it as she continued.

"You're Ms. P. Carlisle." Giles nodded as he saw the small print beneath the name.

He was so excited about getting to Colorado for a snowy, cold Christmas that he'd missed that. It was not like Giles to miss things like that.

"Yes, I am," Priscilla confirmed. "The new owners of the lodge are my grandchildren." She informed him. "They're unaware of Avery's plans, but I'm not. Today, I asked her if she'd had a response from you, and she said no." There was a pause as if she was waiting for him to reply. "As time is short, I'd like to know your answer or make other plans."

"Before I answer that question," Giles said, sitting back in his chair. "I need to ask why you haven't invested in the lodge if it's dire."

"Because I have stubborn grandchildren," Priscilla told him. "They want to do everything on their own. But I intend to step in if you're not interested in investing, which would disappoint me given your reputation."

Giles smiled. He liked Priscilla. She didn't mince her words, and he liked that her grandchildren didn't want to be spoon-fed by their super-wealthy grandparent.

"As you called, I was making arrangements to get to Frisco in two days," Giles told her. "I am interested in investing in the lodge. Avery seems very passionate about it, and I trust her instincts."

"I couldn't agree with you more, Mr. Holland," Priscilla agreed.

"Please, call me Giles," Giles said. "My assistant is trying to find accommodation for me."

"Please tell her not to worry about accommodation," Priscilla told him. "I have a cabin at the lodge for you that I'm sure you'll find quite adequate."

"Thank you." Giles closed the folder. "I'll be there tomorrow."

"Could I make a suggestion about your arrival?" Priscilla asked.

"Okay!" Giles frowned.

"I would like to meet you before you arrive at the lodge." Priscilla's voice lowered, and he could hear voices around her. "Could you fly into Denver, and we meet there? My driver can take us to the lodge together the next day."

"Okay," Giles answered. "But I have a helicopter to take us to the lodge the following day."

"That's even better for me." Priscilla laughed. "I haven't been in one of those for years."

Giles took the details to meet Priscilla. After the call, he sat staring at the phone for a few seconds, a feeling growing inside him that he was about to embark on an adventure that would change his life forever.

CHAPTER THREE

Heather woke up in her grandmother's cozy cottage in Frisco, the anticipation of the day ahead stirring in her chest. Today, she would accompany her enigmatic grandmother, Priscilla, on a two-day trip to Denver. Priscilla had some business in Denver and was being cagey and secretive about it, but Heather shook it off. She'd grown up with her grandmother and was used to her not discussing her business affairs.

Heather reminded herself that she wasn't being forthright about her reason for offering to go with her grandmother to Denver. She had pretended it was to buy Christmas gifts as it was four days to Christmas, and Heather hadn't done her shopping. But she'd managed to book a last-minute appointment with a doctor in Denver that Heather's Los Angeles doctor had recommended. Heather was due for a checkup on her leg. As her family didn't know about her injury, she wasn't going to tell them. Well, not until after Christmas.

Especially when everyone was having such fun, and there was a hint of rekindled romance between Ryder and Avery.

Heather wouldn't be a Debbie downer and tell the story of her injury to her family just yet, if at all. If they didn't need to know, why make a big deal of something that happened in the past?

Heather went about her routine as the morning light filtered through the curtains. She showered, dressed, and packed a small overnight bag with essentials. After packing, Heather went from the cottage to the grand lodge. With its rustic charm, the lodge's main building was bustling with guests and staff.

Heather needed to find Emily. She wanted to tell Emily she wouldn't be joining them on their shopping trip the following day.

"Hi, do you know where Emily is?" Heather asked the concierge.

"Emily left for Frisco early this morning," the concierge said, "But Ryder should be around here somewhere."

"Thanks." Heather frowned and went to look for Ryder.

Heather found Ryder loading their grandmother's overnight bag into the back of the town car.

"Ryder," Heather greeted him with a warm smile. "Good morning."

Ryder looked up from his task. "Morning, Heather. I believe you're going with Gran to Denver."

"Yes," Heather confirmed. "I was actually looking for Emily. I wanted to let her know that I won't be able to go shopping in Silverthorne with them tomorrow."

Ryder held out his hands for her bag, which she handed him.

"I'll let her know," Ryder told her, putting Heather's bag next to their grandmother's before closing the trunk. "Do you know what Gran's urgent business in Denver is?"

"Not a clue," Heather answered, shaking her head.

"Why are you going with her?" Ryder asked, his eyes narrowing suspiciously.

"I haven't done any Christmas shopping," Heather told him. It wasn't a lie. She really did need to get some presents for the family. "There's not much in Frisco, and I was going to take a shuttle to Denver anyway."

"I guess there are no big shopping malls in the Arctic." Ryder turned as their grandmother walked out of the lodge, as well groomed and dressed as always.

"Ah, there you are, Heather." Priscilla slipped on her leather gloves as she walked toward them, saving Heather from answering Ryder. "Are you ready to go?"

"I am." Heather nodded.

She glanced at her casual attire of jeans, cotton shirt, sneakers, and bomber jacket, suddenly feeling underdressed compared to her grandmother. Regarding grooming, Priscilla looked like a make-up artist had groomed her. Heather had no make-up on, and her hair was scraped back in a casual ponytail.

"Then we'd best be on our way," Priscilla instructed as their driver opened the backdoor of the vehicle for them. "Goodbye, sweetheart." She kissed Ryder's cheeks before sliding into the car.

"I don't suppose you'll let me know what she's up to if you find out?" Ryder whispered to Heather.

"I'll try to find out," Heather whispered back. "But you know Gran. She's as cagey as anything."

"Thanks, anything you can find out." Ryder frowned worriedly. "I think she's up to something, and I have a feeling it's got something to do with the lodge."

"Sure." Heather nodded and climbed in next to her grandmother. She looked up at Ryder as he was about to close the door. "Don't forget to tell Emily I'm gone."

"I won't," Ryder assured her, closing the car door.

The car pulled away and drove down the long driveway past the festival, where the booth owners were getting ready for the day.

"I'm so glad the festival has been such a success," Heather commented as they pulled onto the road leading them to Denver.

"Yes, it has been," Priscilla replied, pulling documents from her briefcase. "Sorry, dear, but I have some paperwork to review before we arrive in Denver." She looked at Heather. "Do you have something to pass the time?"

"Yes, I'm going to sleep," Heather said and grinned.

Heather reached for her phone, slipped in her earphones, and selected her beloved animal-themed show. She settled into the car's plush, warm leather seats, wrapping herself in a cozy cocoon. It didn't take long for the soothing hum of the engine and the gentle cadence of the drive to lull her into a peaceful slumber.

As the car rolled to a stop, the soft murmur of the city coming to life outside slowly penetrated Heather's consciousness. She stirred in her seat, and her grandmother's gentle hand on her shoulder roused her from her nap.

"Heather, dear, we've arrived at the Fairmont Hotel," Priscilla announced.

Heather blinked her eyes open, momentarily disoriented by the abrupt change in surroundings. The polished elegance of the luxurious five-star hotel greeted them, and a uniformed valet hurried over to assist with their luggage.

Heather and Priscilla checked in, and a discreet concierge

led them to their opulent two-bedroom suite, adorned with lavish furnishings and floor-to-ceiling windows that offered a panoramic view of the city.

Heather went to her room and selected a comfortable outfit for her doctor's appointment. Flowing pants, a loose blouse, and slip-on shoes would ensure the doctor had easy access to her leg. She decided to do her hair and makeup on an impulsive whim, knowing she had some time to spare before the appointment. She put extra effort into her appearance, enhancing her features and adding a touch of vibrancy to her outfit. It was the festive season, and Heather never really got the opportunity to doll herself up, and what better excuse to do that than Christmas shopping?

When Heather returned to the living room area of their suite, her grandmother had also changed into what she called her business attire. Priscilla looked sharp and professional in a tailored pantsuit, her presence exuding an air of authority and confidence.

"You're looking smarter than usual, Gran." Heather grinned.

"I can say the same about you, dear." Priscilla ran an eye over Heather's appearance. "You should make this kind of effort more often, sweetheart, as you look stunning."

"Thank you, Gran," Heather replied and checked her wristwatch. "I'm going to call a cab and get stuck into some Christmas shopping." She walked over to the hotel phone and asked for a cab. When she was done, she hung up and turned to Pricilla. "Anything special you want for Christmas, Gran?"

"No, honey, I have everything I need." Priscilla sat on the sofa with the folder she'd been going over in the car. "My family is all together this year."

"Yes, but what would you like, or else I'm just going to get you one of those gifts you don't want and feel obliged to keep." Heather sighed dramatically. "Then I'm going to feel bad for aiding you in becoming a serial hoarder."

Priscilla laughed at Heather's silliness. "I would like an animal brooch to add to the collection you send me yearly."

"What if I can't find one of those this year?" Heather felt a cold sweat pop out on her brow.

She usually custom-designed a unique animal brooch for her grandmother as a Christmas tradition, each representing an animal she had worked with throughout the year. However, this year, Heather found herself both short on time and reluctant to continue the tradition. Deep down, she recognized that her hesitation was rooted in an underlying fear that had taken hold after the jaguar incident. But Heather refused to let this newfound apprehension dominate her. She had always been fearless and was determined not to let a minor scratch on her leg instill a fear of jaguars.

Her mind screamed a reminder that it was not a little scratch and nearly ended her life, but Heather pushed her thoughts and fears aside. She'd find a jeweler with a jaguar brooch or crystal statue. Heather liked the idea of a statue because her grandmother had enough pins from her. Maybe her grandmother could start a crystal statue collection this year. Priscilla loved crystal statues.

"I'll love whatever you get me." Priscilla smiled warmly at Heather before turning back to her documents.

"What's on your agenda for the day, Gran?" Heather flopped on the sofa beside Priscilla, hoping to get a sneak peek at the documents.

"I have a business meeting at eleven-thirty," Priscilla explained. "It's an early lunch meeting."

Heather chuckled, her eyes twinkling with mischief. "Early lunch? Sounds more like a brunch meeting, Gran."

Priscilla rolled her eyes good-naturedly. "Semantics, my dear."

Heather was just about to glimpse the documents when Priscilla's phone rang, and she closed the folder to get her phone. Heather took that as her cue to leave. She leaned in and kissed Priscilla's cheek before leaving the suite to wait for her cab.

Heather had left the suite and was making her way to the elevator. Her heels clicked rhythmically on the polished marble floor of the hotel. As she approached the elevator, her fingers hit the down button to call the elevator. Her mind ticked over what she needed to get done after her doctor's appointment.

The elevator gave a soft ding before the doors slid open, and she stepped in. Heather was just about to press the button for the foyer when she heard a voice echo from down the hallway.

"Hold the elevator, please."

Startled, Heather looked up to see a tall, handsome man striding toward her. His charcoal-gray business suit was clearly designer, exuding an air of sophistication and affluence. With a swift and graceful movement, she extended her arm to stop the elevator doors from closing.

"Sure," she replied, a friendly smile on her face as she noticed only two suites on this floor, and this impeccably dressed man was likely the guest in the other one. Her curiosity piqued, she glanced at him briefly.

The man entered the elevator with a grateful nod. He was undeniably good-looking, with sharp features and an air of confidence that was both intriguing and slightly intimidating.

As the doors closed, he glanced at Heather and then at the elevator panel.

"Ground floor?" he inquired, his voice smooth and cultured.

Heather almost gave her usual cheeky response but caught herself in time, instead opting for a polite nod. "Yes, I'm heading to the ground floor."

Their elevator ride was silent for a moment. The only sound was the soft hum as it descended. Heather couldn't help but feel a strange connection with this man. It wasn't just his good looks but something about him that tugged at her subconscious. The closer he'd gotten, the stronger the feeling had become, making her unconsciously shift slightly away from him.

He cleared his throat, breaking the silence. "Are you a guest at the Fairmont?" he inquired politely. His blue eyes met hers.

Heather hesitated briefly, once again biting down on the sarcastic remark that had instantly sprung to her tongue. "Yes, I am. And you?"

The man looked at her as if he was surprised by her question, and she'd somehow know he was. Although Heather pretty much knew he was. There was no way an employee of the hotel could afford the clothes he was wearing, let alone the watch on his arm.

"Yes." The man nodded. "I have suit number one on the floor where we met."

"Ah." Heather nodded, and their eyes met once again.

Heather felt a strange jolt of energy pass between them. She quickly looked away, focusing on the slowly lighting numbers above the elevator doors. Before they could exchange any more pleasantries, the elevator landed at the designated floor, and the doors opened.

The man politely stepped back so Heather could exit first.

"Have a nice day," the man said, with a nod before walking toward the concierge and before Heather could reply.

She stood there for a few seconds, watching the man converse with the woman. The doorman approached her, reminding her that her cab was waiting. Heather thanked him and turned to take one last look at the man who'd shared the elevator with her, but he had vanished like a fleeting figment of her imagination. Heather frowned, feeling an odd sense of disappointment, which she couldn't quite explain. Shaking off this strange reaction, she turned towards the exit to catch her cab.

Heather breathed in the crisp winter air as she exited the medical center. She'd just endured three hours of scans and a thorough examination. The doctor wasn't particularly pleased with how red and inflamed the scar on Heather's leg looked from the recent cut that ran through it.

Reluctantly, Heather had told the doctor that the cut resulted from a nail at one of the booths she'd helped assemble for the Mistletoe Winter Festival. The doctor had given her a disapproving look, akin to the one a parent gives a child who hasn't listened, before asking if she'd sought medical attention immediately. Heather had responded with an eye roll before further explaining that she had cleaned the wound with disinfectant and applied a band-aid, which only deepened the doctor's disapproving glare.

Heather sighed in frustration as she buttoned up her coat and pulled on her snug leather gloves. If the infection didn't subside from the prescribed medication and cream, the thought of more potential tests was disheartening. She shook her head to dispel these worries, taking another lungful of the crisp winter air. The cool breeze had a revitalizing quality that momentarily eased her concerns.

Making her way towards her shopping destination, Heather recalled the nurse at the clinic who had suggested she go shopping in the area. The festive street mall she was headed to was nestled among charming boutiques, and at the far end, there was a larger shopping mall. The prospect of a delightful shopping experience helped brighten her mood, and she looked forward to finding unique Christmas gifts for her family.

It was late afternoon, and Heather was laden with gifts as she waited patiently for her cab to arrive outside the shopping mall at the end of the festive street mall. Heather noticed a drugstore across the road as her taxi pulled up and remembered she had to fill her prescription.

"Can I help you with those?" The cab driver climbed out of the car and put her parcels in the trunk.

"Would you mind waiting for me while I go across the street?" Heather pointed to the drugstore. "I have to get a prescription filled."

"No problem," the cab driver assured her.

Heather rushed across the street, and thankfully, hardly anyone was in the store. It didn't take long for the pharmacist to get her order ready. Heather rushed toward the door, and at the same time, a man with his attention caught by his phone walked in. She tried to step out of his way, but there wasn't a lot of room in the small store, and he walked into her.

"Watch out!" Heather said through gritted teeth and sucked in her breath when the man raised his head, and her eyes collided with the blue ones of the man from the elevator.

"I'm sorry," the man said and frowned when he saw her. "Oh, hello again."

"You know you shouldn't walk and text," Heather told him, her eyes transfixed on his.

"I don't usually," the man said, pocketing the device. "But I'm in the middle of a time-sensitive business transaction."

"Still, you're lucky I wasn't a fragile old lady or small kid," Heather pointed out. "You could've seriously hurt them by knocking into them."

"Noted." The man nodded. His eyes sparkled with amusement. "But then again, by the force of our impact, you must've been moving pretty fast and not fully aware of your surroundings either."

"I have a cab waiting for me with the meter running," Heather excused her actions and broke eye contact by looking to see if the cab was still waiting for her.

The man stepped to one side to allow her access to the door.

"Don't let me keep you then." The man smiled at her. "It was nice to run into you again."

"Let's hope it's the last time." Heather gave him a tight smile. "Have a nice evening, Number One."

With that, she stepped out the door. Her heart was doing crazy jolting movements while her nervous system was zinging and forcing the butterflies in her stomach to flap about while her knees felt like jelly. Heather gave herself a mental shake and walked over to her cab to take her back to the Fairmont Hotel to meet her grandmother for dinner.

CHAPTER FOUR

Giles strode confidently through the elegant foyer of the Fairmont Hotel. The evening had settled in, casting a warm glow over the luxurious surroundings. He was on his way to meet Priscilla Carlisle for dinner at the hotel's upscale restaurant, and the anticipation hung in the air.

Today, Giles had found their brunch meeting quite agreeable. Priscilla Carlisle had laid out a compelling proposal for him to invest in Mistletoe Lodge, and their discussions had left him keen on the idea. Tomorrow, they'd be flying back to Mistletoe Lodge in his luxurious helicopter, the Pegasus II, a sleek chariot of the skies that matched his opulent lifestyle. He had a few of them that were housed in cities where he had offices, like Denver.

Priscilla had also invited him to dine with her and her granddaughter, an explorer and conservationist he had yet to meet. Giles couldn't help but sigh inwardly at the thought. While he wholeheartedly supported conservation efforts, his past encounters with conservationists had often left a bitter taste. They were usually after his money, and he was already a patron of numerous charitable organizations. But his conversation with Priscilla had somehow left him more enthusiastic about investing in the lodge. The prospect of seeing the place firsthand was an alluring thought, and so he begrudgingly agreed to endure dinner with Priscilla's conservationist granddaughter.

Giles's thoughts briefly veered back to the spirited woman with fiery golden hair and jewel-green eyes he'd bumped into earlier that day. A smile tugged at his lips at the memory. He hoped to have the chance to run into her again before his departure the following day. There was an inexplicable attraction that had been ignited, and he was eager to introduce himself to her.

As Giles reached the restaurant entrance, his eyes swept the room, but Priscilla was nowhere in sight. He was just about to provide the restaurant manager with the reservation name when, out of the blue, the woman who had occupied his thoughts all day appeared at his side.

Both were taken aback by the unexpected reunion, and she greeted him playfully. "Hello, Number One. We really have to stop meeting this way."

Before they could exchange any further words, Giles's attention was abruptly stolen by the arrival of Priscilla, who rushed into the restaurant with an apologetic air.

"I'm sorry I'm late," Priscilla said, then paused. She looked from Giles to the fiery-haired, green-eyed vixen beside him. "Oh, good, I see you two have met."

"I beg your pardon?" Giles's brow creased, and his heart jolted as he stared stupidly at Priscilla.

"My granddaughter," Pricilla pointed to the woman beside him.

"You know Number One?" The green-eyed woman spluttered and pointed to Giles.

"Yes, I invited Giles to dine with us," Priscilla told her.

"Grandmother," the woman teased. "Is this the reason you were so cagey about your *business trip?*" A grin spread across her beautiful lips, and the smile put a twinkle in her eyes. "I'm getting a new grandfather for Christmas."

"Don't be vulgar, sweetheart," Priscilla raised her eyebrows and shook her head at the woman. "Giles is a business colleague."

Only then did it finally sink in for Giles that the woman who'd tormented his thoughts the entire day was Priscilla's conservationist granddaughter! He couldn't help but look at the woman in shock as she faced her grandmother.

"Giles?" the woman frowned, her head swiveling toward him. "As in Giles Holland?"

"Yes, that would be me," Giles replied with a slight nod and a slightly narrowed gaze.

"Oh, sorry, Giles," Priscilla returned their attention to her. "I thought the two of you had already met." She introduced her granddaughter. "This is my granddaughter, Heather."

The two of them looked at each other, confusion etching Giles's features. However, Heather's expression conveyed disdain, a look Giles didn't expect. Their silent interaction was interrupted by the hostess.

"Mrs. Carlisle, how lovely to see you again," the hostess beamed as she greeted Priscilla. "I have your table ready for you."

"Thank you." Priscilla gracefully stepped around Giles and Heather, following the hostess to their table.

Giles politely held back, gesturing for Heather to precede him. Once they were seated, small talk ensued as they awaited the server to take their orders. Heather turned to her grandmother as the server vanished into the bustling restaurant.

"What business do you and Giles have?" Heather inquired. Her tone was laced with suspicion.

"Giles is a good friend of Avery's," Priscilla explained, her voice calm and measured. "She's trying to help save the lodge from being taken over by a large spa and resort chain."

"Avery asked me if I'd be interested in investing in Mistletoe Lodge," Giles added. He felt an unexpected compulsion to provide some clarity to Heather, though he wasn't entirely sure why.

When Giles first realized that the woman he'd been captivated by all day had recognized him as Giles Holland, he'd felt a sinking disappointment, but that feeling had quickly dissipated. However, Heather's reaction to the mention of his name was somewhat puzzling. The look in her eyes and the way she'd said his name led Giles to believe she hadn't known who he was during their initial meeting earlier in the day.

Twice, Giles reminded himself. *I met Heather twice today*.

Now, he was perplexed about why she seemed to harbor disdain toward him. His frown deepened as he contemplated how someone with access to modern forms of communication could remain oblivious to his identity. It then dawned on him that Priscilla had mentioned earlier that day that her granddaughter frequently traveled to remote areas around the globe and that Heather was away more than she was home in Los Angeles.

"How did you and Avery meet?" Heather inquired. Her eyes fixed intently on Giles.

"We met at UCLA," Giles replied. "Over the years, we've worked together on several investment projects."

Heather's gaze never wavered as she continued to scrutinize him. Giles felt like he was being interrogated under a harsh spotlight.

"What kind of investments?" she pressed, her tone holding a trace of accusation.

Giles hesitated for a moment, choosing his words carefully. "Mainly, we focus on saving small businesses from being absorbed by larger corporations," he explained.

Heather's eyes narrowed with an accusatory glare. "Didn't you make your fortune by dismantling larger corporations? By conducting hostile takeovers and then breaking down the organization, selling it off piece by piece?" She arched an eyebrow. "So, instead of the big fish swallowing the small one, you were the smaller fish taking bites out of the bigger one until there was nothing left."

The venom in Heather's voice caught Giles off guard, making him wonder what he had done to provoke such disdain from her. Her sharp words pierced through the air.

"Heather!" Priscilla hissed, fixing her granddaughter with a warning look. "That's no way to speak to our guest."

Heather's gaze remained fixed on Giles as she replied with a tight smile, "He's *your* guest, Gran. If I had known you'd invited Giles Holland to dine with us, I'd have preferred to stay in and order room service."

Giles was momentarily speechless, his brows furrowing as he struggled to comprehend her inexplicable animosity directed at him. Finally, he gathered his composure and decided to address the situation.

"Excuse me, but have I done something to upset you?" Giles asked Heather. The surprise he felt was palpable in his voice. He was taken aback by her fierce hostility but was determined not to allow it to go unexplained.

Heather's beautiful eyes darkened with anger as she responded with an edge to her voice, "It's not just about me."

"Care to elaborate?" Giles watched her.

Heather clenched her jaw, her anger evident as she leaned slightly forward in her chair. Her voice, while filled with frustration, retained a tinge of sadness. "I should've known you wouldn't remember, Mr. Giles Holland. Clean water is like air to you, so why would you care about the African Wildlife and Rural Village Conservation project to bring clean water to the people and animals in Central Africa?"

Giles's brows knitted together as he tried to recall any such project. "I'm afraid I don't recall that specific project," he admitted with a hint of remorse.

Heather's words grew sharper as she continued, "That's because you pulled your foundation's funding from the project as it got started. The project would have provided fresh water to the villagers and the animals in a few rural villages. When your foundation pulled out, the project fell apart. A lot of people and endangered animals died." She swallowed, Giles saw her struggling with her emotions, and her voice dipped. "I lost some good people because of that."

Giles leaned back, his face a canvas of distress. "I don't handle the day-to-day operations of my foundations. I rely on a team of experts to make such decisions. If something like that happened, it was without my knowledge. I would never support pulling from a project if it would cause harm."

Giles's confusion grew. He knew all his foundations, but he couldn't recall that one.

Heather's anger softened to a simmering disappointment as she responded, "Whether you knew or not, the damage was done. That project meant everything to us. I've seen the suffering it caused firsthand." She shook her head as she stared at him in disgust. "Luckily, a few local farmers got together to help. But because of limited resources, the project took longer, and the dam wasn't as big as it was supposed to be."

Priscilla observed the heated exchange between her grand-daughter and her guest with a somber expression, realizing the source of the tension. Giles realized that the situation weighed heavily on Heather's heart, and her apparent connection to it had bred an unshakable anger toward Giles.

Giles sighed, running a hand through his hair. "I can't apologize enough for any involvement my foundation may have had in causing that harm. I'll investigate the matter and ensure such mistakes aren't repeated."

Heather's gaze never softened, even at the remorse Giles conveyed. He could only imagine how the memory of the suffering endured by the villagers and animals still haunted her. Suddenly, Giles knew he didn't want to be the source of her pain. And it wouldn't help the project, but he'd ensure a thorough investigation. If there were anything to save or still to be done, Giles would make darn sure it would be.

"Investigate all you want, but it won't change what happened," she replied, her voice tinged with sadness. "The villagers may not have been a business, but the new dam was supposed to help with agriculture for them to grow their own produce." She shook her head.

Giles nodded solemnly, and their conversation was interrupted as the server returned with their meals. They ate in stilted silence—the air heavy with unspoken words and unresolved issues. As dinner continued, Priscilla picked up the conversation about Mistletoe Lodge.

"You're arriving in time for the Winter Festival Christmas Ball tomorrow night, Giles," Priscilla took a sip of water. "The ball is already sold out, but I've reserved a ticket for you."

"Thank you. I appreciate that." Giles forced a smile for Priscilla.

"Maybe you and Heather can accompany each other." Priscilla raised an eyebrow as she glanced from Heather to Giles.

"I'm sorry, Gran," Heather replied. "As you know, I don't like balls and hadn't planned on going."

"Nonsense!" Priscilla put the water glass down and looked at Heather. "I bought you a beautiful gown this afternoon, especially for the ball."

"Gran!" Heather hissed and rolled her eyes. "I told you I'm not going to it."

"Are your grandson and other granddaughter wanting to make the Winter Festival an annual festival?" Giles changed the subject as he didn't want to anger Heather more than she already was.

"It used to be an annual affair," Priscilla told him. "Until my daughter-in-law passed away, my son stopped having it. My grandchildren, Ryder and Emily, want to bring it back as one, especially after the success of this one."

"I'm glad to hear that," Giles told her, leaning back in his chair after finishing his meal.

The server broke their conversation as he came to take their dishes away, and he saw Priscilla rub her temples.

"I don't think I'm going to make dessert," Priscilla informed them. "I'm coming down with a headache."

"Can I get you something?" Giles offered. His voice filled with concern.

"Oh, no, I'll be fine," Pricilla assured him. "Nothing, a hot shower, and sleep won't fix."

"I'll go with you," Heather said, and Giles felt disappointment zap through him.

"No, you should stay and have dessert and maybe a coffee." Priscilla raised an eyebrow and looked from Heather to Giles. "Maybe it will sweeten you up so you and Giles can settle your differences." Heather was about to say something, but Pricilla held her hand up, silencing her. "It's Christmas, and as Giles is with us at the lodge for the next three weeks, I suggest you find a way to resolve your issue with him."

"It's going to take much more than dessert," Heather muttered, eliciting a stern glance from her grandmother.

"Goodnight, Giles." Priscilla smiled warmly at him. She patted Heather's shoulder, saying, "I'll see you in the morning for breakfast." Priscilla leaned down to kiss Heather on the cheek.

Heather sighed in resignation. "Goodnight, Gran."

As Priscilla left the restaurant and her footsteps faded into the distance, Heather and Giles exchanged hesitant glances. The heavy atmosphere of their earlier exchange hung around them, an uncomfortable silence settling in the restaurant. It was as if the walls were bracing themselves for an impending storm.

Giles decided to break the stifling silence after they ordered dessert. "Heather, which of my foundations was responsible for financing the project you mentioned earlier?"

Heather met his gaze with a cool, unwavering stare. "The foundation was named the Wildlife Guardians Foundation. Your organization funded it and supported a project to build a dam in a remote village to provide water for the local wildlife and the villagers."

Giles' brow furrowed as he tried to recall that foundation. The name didn't resonate, and he grew increasingly concerned about the situation. He leaned forward slightly. His interest piqued. "Can you tell me who the main contact was for the foundation?"

Heather's expression remained stern as she replied, "Gordon Jackson."

Giles' confusion deepened as he struggled to recall any details about the foundation. The name Gordon Jackson meant nothing to him, and he felt disoriented by the unfolding conversation. He continued probing, trying to get more information. "You wouldn't happen to be able to retrieve some of the foundation's information for me, would you?"

Heather leaned back, still keeping a watchful eye on Giles. "Yes, I have all the documentation filed in my email."

Giles was genuinely perplexed by this revelation. The more Heather disclosed, the more his memories failed to align with the situation. However, he chose to keep his confusion hidden and maintained a neutral tone. "I would like to follow up on this matter."

Heather regarded him with skepticism and asked, "And then what?"

Giles was quick to respond, emphasizing his intent to

resolve the matter. "Heather, I assure you that I would never have withdrawn funding from a project of such magnitude, especially one carrying those risks. I can't fathom how I was unaware of this project, which concerns me deeply. I prefer to keep a vigilant eye on my foundations and their work."

Heather's eyes remained fixed on him. Her distrust was still evident. He continued, "I would like the chance to investigate this situation thoroughly. The damage to the villages and wildlife is deplorable, and the potential implications could point to a fraudulent foundation operating under my company's name."

The tension between them remained palpable, but the conversation had shifted from hostility to an uneasy alliance. Heather's skepticism hadn't dissipated entirely, but the prospect of uncovering the truth had shifted the dynamics of their interaction.

"I will provide you with all the documents and information you need," Heather told him, her tone more accommodating as their coffee and dessert arrived. "The dam project aimed to provide a sustainable water source for the endangered wildlife and the villagers suffering from a severe water shortage after an outbreak of Leptospirosis." Her eyes darkened as she spoke. "The water they did have wasn't safe for consumption. The dam was supposed to be their lifeline, a fresh start, and a better future."

Giles listened intently, realizing the gravity of the situation. "Thank you." He gave her a tight smile. "I promise you as soon as I have all the information, I'll launch an investigation."

Heather nodded and continued to explain, "When the funding was pulled and the project stalled, the dam was left incomplete. This unfortunate timing coincided with a period of heavy rainfall. The dam was meant to capture and store this rainwater, ensuring a clean water source for the villagers and the wildlife. However, because it remained unfinished, the heavy rainfall washed away the partially constructed dam, and the torrential water mixed with the contaminated sources, worsening the situation. It resulted in villagers and animals consuming the polluted water."

Giles could sense the urgency in Heather's voice, and her explanation painted a clearer picture of the devastation caused by the stalled project. As he listened, he was struck by the enormity of the consequences of the foundation's actions, or lack thereof.

The tension between them started to lessen as they finished their desserts. Giles realized there was much more to Heather than he'd first realized when Priscilla told him about her granddaughter. She wasn't just any conservationist. Heather was genuinely passionate about her work and, from what he could gather, actively involved.

They ordered a sherry after their dessert, and Giles realized he wasn't ready for the evening to end.

"How did you get involved in conservation?" Giles asked her.

"It's kind of become part of my job," Heather told him.

"What is the other part of your job?" Giles took a sip of sherry.

"I'm a wildlife veterinarian," Heather's reply surprised him, and he nearly choked.

"Really?" Giles's eyes widened.

"You look surprised." Heather raised an eyebrow.

"Your grandmother told me you were an explorer and

conservationist," Giles explained. "She didn't mention you were a veterinarian."

"She leaves that part out a lot." Heather laughed, and just like that, the rich, warm sound of her laughter shattered the tension that formed a barrier around them. "When I told her I wanted to study medicine, she hoped I meant human medicine."

"I think what you do is admirable," Giles told her honestly. "There couldn't be too many wildlife vets as I wouldn't imagine too many people would want to examine a large predator."

He saw something flash in her eyes that looked like fear, but it was fleeting, and he thought he could have mistaken the look.

"We have good tranquilizers that enable us to get up close and personal with the largest and fiercest animals." She turned her sherry glass on the table in front of her. "Looking after wildlife seems to progress into conservation naturally." She shrugged. "For me, anyway."

"I have to say I've met many people with the most amazing jobs, including a Lego engineer." He smiled at the look of surprise at that. "But you're the first wildlife vet I've met."

"You've met a Lego engineer?" Heather looked at him amazed, and whatever tension lingered around them dissolved as soon as she admitted. "I love Lego, and it's been like a bucket list item of mine to meet a Lego engineer."

"I think the way Lego sets are designed is fascinating," Giles told her.

"Me too!" Heather agreed, and at first, he thought she was joking with him, but the light in her eyes told him she wasn't kidding.

"Are you serious?" Giles frowned.

"I am." Heather nodded and whipped out her phone. Flipping through it, she turned the screen to him. "This is my Jurassic Park set."

"Oh wow." Giles took her phone. "Who is that young boy with you?" He handed her phone back.

"He was one of the villagers in India when I was there helping a tiger conservation organization." Heather took her phone. "My grandmother knows how much I've always loved Lego, and when she knows I'm going on an assignment, she always sends me a new set to do while I'm away." She grinned. "It's become a thing with my team now, and I donate the sets to village kids, hospitals, and so on when I'm done. Sometimes, the village kids like to help me with them."

"That's amazing." Giles took another sip of sherry, feeling his heart slowly being lost to the incredible woman in front of him.

CHAPTER FIVE

As Heather and Giles continued to sip their sherry, the initial tension that had hung over their conversation began to dissolve. In the cozy restaurant, their stories flowed freely, and the soft, ambient music added to the comfortable backdrop of their discussion.

Curiosity got the best of Heather, and she decided to inquire about Giles's relationship with Avery. "Tell me more about how you and Avery met," she asked, genuinely interested in the backstory.

Giles leaned back in his chair, a nostalgic smile playing on his lips. "It all began about twelve years ago when we started at UCLA. We were typical clueless freshmen and met on the first day of class. I remember we were trying to navigate the labyrinthine campus, hopelessly lost. Fortunately, we ran into another student, a lifesaver really, named Ashley."

Heather nodded, recalling her own early experiences at large campuses. "UCLA can be quite a maze if you're unfamiliar with it."

Giles laughed, nodding. "Absolutely. And thanks to Ashley, we found our way to class in the nick of time."

"Ashley?" Heather's brows furrowed. The name sounded familiar, and she wondered if this was the same Ashley she had heard Avery mention years ago.

"Yes, Ashley Forsythe," Giles confirmed. "She was a key part of our dynamic trio. At first, I had quite the crush on Avery." He chuckled. "But our relationship never took a romantic turn. We became close friends instead."

Heather found herself intrigued. "Just friends?"

Giles smiled at her question. "Yes, just friends. Avery was heartbroken back then, and it took her years to recover. I'm not entirely convinced it ever fully did."

Giles's apparent affection for Avery made Heather experience a mix of emotions, one she couldn't quite put a finger on. "You care deeply for her, don't you?"

"Yes," Giles admitted, his tone softening. "I care for Avery and Ashley deeply. They're an important part of my life."

Heather shifted the topic away from Avery's romantic life. "Did you say Ashley Forsythe?" Her eyes narrowed questioningly. "As in Ashley Forsythe, the fashion and beauty mogul?"

Giles's face lit up. "Yes. She's the one. Although the three of us aren't in constant touch like before, we're still close friends. I actually saw her about a week ago at her annual Christmas Ball."

Heather let out an exaggerated groan. "The dreaded formal ball. My Gran and her family are always invited to that thing."

Giles chuckled, appreciating Heather's honesty. "You weren't kidding about your aversion to formal events."

Heather sipped her sherry, the rich flavors settling comfortably on her palate. "No, I'd take on an angry polar bear any day over attending one."

Giles laughed, appreciating her candidness. "Is that what you were doing in the Arctic?" He teased her. "Facing down a polar bear to escape a formal event."

"More like escaping the entire festive season." Heather grinned, feeling a warm flush of camaraderie. "I prefer the raw and unpredictable over the polished and pretentious."

Giles leaned forward. His gaze was curious. "Have you faced down a polar bear?"

Heather's eyes sparkled as she shared her story. "I wouldn't say facing one down. The bear was tranquilized."

Giles was genuinely intrigued. "That's remarkable. I imagine being a wildlife vet presents its unique challenges."

"You can't imagine," Heather replied, her voice brimming with enthusiasm. "There's something incredibly special about working with these magnificent creatures. It's thrilling and sometimes nerve-wracking."

He leaned forward, captivated by her tales. "I bet it's both rewarding and challenging, too."

Heather felt a sense of ease wash over her as she shared the details of her work. As the evening continued, they delved into a deeper conversation, with their connection growing stronger and Heather's skepticism gradually melting away. The warm atmosphere and Giles's genuine interest made her feel more comfortable around him.

The restaurant continued to buzz with activity, but in their own corner, it felt as if it was just the two of them, sharing stories and forming a connection that was slowly but surely changing Heather's initial skepticism into genuine curiosity and a desire to get to know Giles better.

As Heather and Giles continued to sip their sherry, their conversation deepened, and they found themselves getting to know each other better. The restaurant's cozy ambiance created a sense of intimacy that went beyond their initial skepticism.

"May I ask about your parents?" Giles sat back, watching her intently.

"I can't really remember them," Heather admitted. "They died when I was four. They were coming home from work on a rainy night. A drunk driver skidded across the oncoming lane and hit them."

"That's awful." Giles's eyes filled with compassion. "I'm sorry."

"I grew up with my gran." Heather smiled. "I can remember being heartbroken at the time. "I wasn't lacking for love or attention as I had it in droves from my grandmother and grandfather before they split."

"They got divorced?" Giles's brow creased.

"No, they never got divorced." Heather smiled. "They separated, and I became a grandchild of separation." She sipped the sherry. "What about your parents?"

"We have something in common there," Giles told her. "My biological mother left me at a fire station when I was four."

"Seriously?" Heather's eyes widened in disbelief.

"Yup!" Giles nodded. "But it was the best thing she could've done for me." He gave her a tight smile. "I looked into her when I got older and had the resources to do so. She died of an overdose two years after leaving me at the fire station."

"I'm sorry, Giles," was all Heather could think of to say. What did you say to something like that?

"I didn't know." Giles shrugged. "I hardly remember that time except that I spent much of it with my aunt. After she died of cancer, my biological mother took me to the fire station."

"That's heartbreaking!" Heather's voice dropped, and her heart went out to him.

"The man who became my father, Patrick Holland, took me home, and his wife took an instant liking to me, and they became my parents." Giles smiled fondly, thinking about his parents.

Heather listened attentively to Giles's story. "It sounds like fate brought you to them."

Giles smiled, his eyes reflecting deep gratitude. "It certainly seems that way. I've always felt blessed to have them as my parents."

Heather appreciated Giles's kind words. "My grandmother has been my pillar of strength. She's a true force of nature."

Giles found himself admiring Heather's resilience and passion. "Your grandmother is an incredible woman."

Heather nodded, her eyes shining with pride. "She truly is and continues to be a guiding light in my life."

"I feel the same way about my parents," Giles told her. "We lived on a block in Los Angeles that was across the road from the sea. Back then, it was a family neighborhood filled with mom-and-pop type stores, including my mother's bakery." His smile broadened. "We lived in a three-bedroomed apartment on top of it. The building had been in my mother's family for generations."

"That sounds incredible," Heather commented.

"It was." Giles nodded. "We had a big back garden at the back of the bakery and the seaside as my second playground."

"I grew up in Malibu," Heather told him. "Well, before my grandparents split, we'd spend half the year in Malibu and then a couple of months in Frisco because my grandfather had the lodge." She sighed. "When they separated, we moved there permanently. It was my parent's house. It became my house as I inherited it, but my grandmother was my guardian and the executor of my parent's estate."

"I love Malibu," Giles said.

"It's fine," Heather said, giving a nonchalant shrug. "I'm not there much." She gave him a tight smile and shifted the conversation back to him. "Which neighborhood did you live in, in Los Angeles back then?"

"Mar Vista," Giles replied.

Heather's eyes widened with surprise. "That's prime property these days."

Giles clenched his jaw as a flicker of anger passed over his face. "Don't remind me," he said, his eyes darkening with frustration. "When I was a kid, it was a middle-class family neighborhood, one of those places where everyone knew everyone. We used to have street barbecues every Sunday, and there was always some celebration on Saturdays. It was amazing." His eyes flashed with anger. "I was eleven when a development company started buying properties in the neighborhood. They did it sneakily. The bad element infiltrated the streets about eighteen months before the offers started rolling in."

Heather sympathized with his frustration. "How awful! I bet it was the development company. I've heard about this. They bring down the neighborhood to buy up property at a steal."

Giles nodded, his eyes narrowing with anger. "You're absolutely right. My mother and a few others refused to sell. But when the development company couldn't move them, a freak fire swept through part of the street." He sighed. "My mother was forced to sell. Because of how unsafe the neighborhood became, her insurance wasn't enough to cover the damages. She had to sell the building to the development company for half the low price they'd originally offered her. We were forced to move to Downtown Los Angeles, closer to the fire station. We lived in a one-bedroom apartment with a small loft above a Chinese take-out."

Heather's heart went out to him. "Oh, Giles! It sounds like a difficult time."

"When I was sixteen, I got a job at the shop," Giles said, smiling. "Mrs. Chow taught me to cook."

Heather nodded in admiration. "I can boil an egg and cook spaghetti."

Giles laughed. "You also patch up polar bears." He continued his story, saying, "I was in my last year of high school when my father became the Santa Barbara fire station captain. The position came with some great perks, and we moved to a four-bedroom house with a wraparound porch, just like my mother always wanted."

"That's incredible," Heather said, looking at him with newfound appreciation. "I bet your parents live in a nice mansion in Bel Air now."

Giles shook his head. "Nope, they still live in that house in Santa Barbara. My father is now the fire chief, and my mother teaches at a cooking school."

Heather was amazed. "Really?"

Giles confirmed with a nod. "Yes. When I made my first million, I wanted to spoil them, but my parents insisted I invest it because you never know when your fortune will turn the other way."

Heather chuckled. "Your parents sound like wonderful, down-to-earth people."

"They are," Giles said. "And before you ask, I don't have a mansion either."

Heather teasingly asked, "Do you have a superyacht?"

Giles admitted sheepishly, "Okay, that I do. It was my one splurge."

She continued the playful banter. "What about a super-luxurious helicopter?"

"Alright, you caught me," Giles said with a laugh. "So, two splurges. What about you, little Miss Malibu?"

Heather raised her hands in surrender. "My parents left me well off. If it weren't for my eagle-eyed grandmother who manages my money, I'd probably have given it all away to every cause I've ever worked on." She laughed, feeling a flush of embarrassment. "I have to admit I'm not very good with money."

Giles offered some advice. "Then thank goodness for your grandmother. It's admirable that you want to give so much, but you must also be careful not to give too much. You need to keep some back to live on and ensure it makes more money to be able to give more."

Heather nodded, appreciating the wisdom in his words. "That makes sense. I tried to help my cousins with the lodge, but they wouldn't hear of it. I had to try to put money into it in sneaky ways."

"Priscilla said that Emily and Ryder were rather stubborn about not accepting a handout from anyone in the family," Giles recalled.

Heather sighed. Her frustration was evident. "Yeah, Ryder and I had a falling out because he wanted me to sell him my small share in the lodge. But I wouldn't. If I did that, I wouldn't have my small say in it or be able to funnel money into it. Later that year, I voted to sell the lodge, thinking it would be best for Emily and Ryder, allowing them to start fresh. That caused a nuclear fallout between Ryder and myself—he still hasn't forgiven me."

Giles was empathetic. "You were just trying to help. One day, he'll come to his senses and realize that. It's a guy thing. We can't see the forest for the trees."

Heather sighed resignedly before she steered the conversation back to him. "Why aren't you with your parents for Christmas?"

Giles looked forlorn. "They're on a cruise. So, the Mistletoe Lodge deal came through at a good time for me."

Their conversation continued to flow, deepening the connection between them. Heather was slowly discovering that Giles was not just a successful businessman; he had a genuine and compassionate side that drew her in. The evening passed quickly, but neither wanted it to end.

As the evening continued and the restaurant grew quieter, Giles suggested, "How about we continue our conversation at a cozy all-night coffee shop? I know a place nearby that serves amazing festive season hot chocolate." He glanced around the restaurant. "I think they want to close."

Heather's eyes sparkled with enthusiasm. "That sounds perfect. I'd love to." She knew she didn't want the night to end. "Luckily, I have my coat, gloves, and hat."

"Yes, I have mine too," Giles told her. "I came to dinner straight from a meeting."

After they settled the bill, Giles and Heather donned their coats and headed to the nearby coffee shop. It was a refreshing one-block walk from the hotel in the chilly evening air. Inside the cafe, a warm and inviting atmosphere enveloped them. The place was bustling, with customers enjoying the festive season spirit. They were fortunate to discover a cozy booth in a secluded corner.

In the background, a vintage jukebox played a medley of classic tunes, adding a touch of nostalgia to the intimate surroundings. A few couples swayed on the small dance floor nearby, their movements synchronized to the soulful music.

"This is a lovely place," Heather commented, admiring the ambiance.

"It is." Giles nodded in agreement, his eyes reflecting appreciation.

Their pleasant moment was briefly interrupted when a cheerful server approached their table, menus in hand.

"Would you like to hear about our Christmas specials?" The server enquired with an enthusiastic smile.

"Sure." Heather returned the smile.

The server listed the holiday specials, and a particular beverage piqued Heather's interest.

"I'll have the marshmallow peppermint hot chocolate with whipped cream," she said, looking at Giles for his choice.

"Excellent choice," the server complimented, then turned to Giles, her eyes sparkling with anticipation. "And for you?"

Giles contemplated his options for a moment. "Just cocoa for me."

Heather and the server exchanged surprised glances at his choice, then gleefully chimed in unison, "It's Christmas!" They exchanged a high-five for their alike thoughts.

"It's the season to indulge," Heather said, not supporting Giles's choice of beverage.

Giles relented with a resigned sigh. "Fine! Make it two of those marshmallow peppermint drinks."

"Sure thing!" The server nodded with a cheerful grin. "I'll leave the menus with you." She left them with the colorful menu and disappeared to prepare their orders.

Heather couldn't help but tease Giles about his choice. "Were you really going to order plain old cocoa?"

Giles acknowledged his simple preference. "I like cocoa."

With a playful grin, Heather insisted, "Yes, but it tastes much better with added marshmallow and peppermint. You need to be a little more experimental regarding food and beverages. I noticed you had vanilla ice cream for dessert."

Giles chuckled, defending his choice. "I like vanilla ice cream. It's tasty, and you don't get caught up in the millions of other flavors out there and take hours to decide which one to choose. Like good old plain cocoa."

Heather countered, encouraging variety. "Yes, but you're missing out on not trying the other flavors."

Giles looked intrigued and inquired, "What is your favorite flavor of ice cream?"

Heather, grinning mischievously, replied, "There are so many to choose from. When I settle on a favorite, I'll let you know. I tend to go by what I feel like on the day I want ice cream."

Giles, amused by her approach, leaned forward and raised an eyebrow. "I bet that frustrated your grandmother when you were growing up. What if she brought home chocolate ice cream, but your favorite of the day was strawberry?"

Heather leaned back with a self-satisfied expression. "My grandmother never brought home ice cream. Our housekeeper did the shopping, and she always ensured there were a few flavors to choose from. That way, I could mix and make my own flavors."

"Clever." Giles admired her resourcefulness.

Their marshmallow peppermint hot chocolates arrived, and Heather's eyes sparkled with delight as she examined the festive presentation. The steaming mugs were adorned with whipped cream, a candy cane sticking out of the swirled cap, and colorful sprinkles.

Giles took his first sip, his eyes lighting with surprised delight. "It's not bad," he conceded.

Heather, feeling triumphant, couldn't resist correcting him with a playful grin. "I think what you meant to say was, it's delicious."

Giles laughed and took another sip, their conversation gradually transitioning into a comfortable silence.

Heather shifted the conversation back to Giles as they savored their hot chocolates. "You said your parents live in Santa Barbara?" She looked at him curiously. "Do you live close to them?"

Giles put his mug on the table and leaned forward. "I live in Montecito."

Heather playfully teased him. "Of course you do!"

Giles raised an eyebrow, a hint of amusement in his eyes. "What's that supposed to mean? Ah, you think I own a mansion there, don't you? While my house may be larger than average, it's more of a manor house with large gardens."

Heather let out a playful laugh. "A mansion!"

Giles turned the conversation back at her. "What about your house, Miss Malibu?" he inquired, adding a playful twist to the discussion.

Heather kept him guessing about her own home's size and capacity. "It's not too small."

Giles probed further. "How big is it?"

Heather deftly volleyed the question back. "How big is your house?"

Giles laughed, enjoying their lighthearted banter. "Are we playing 'My house is smaller than yours'?"

Heather playfully accepted the challenge. "I bet I'd win, as mine is just a beachfront house with size and height limits. There are strict zoning rules in my area to ensure no obstruction of coastal views, minimal impact on the environment, and to maintain the aesthetic of the coastline."

Giles raised an amused eyebrow. "Did you memorize that?"

Heather admitted with a chuckle, "I did. I wanted to renovate the front deck, and you won't believe the red tape I had to go through."

Giles nodded in understanding. The challenge of home improvement in such areas was not lost on him. "I can imagine."

Suddenly, a slow and melodic song emanated from the jukebox, filling the cafe with a romantic vibe. Wearing a warm and inviting smile, Giles turned the conversation into a personal invitation. "Would you have a dance with me?"

Heather hesitated momentarily, her eyes widening. "I don't dance."

Giles, undeterred, sought clarification. "You can't or don't?"

Their eyes locked, an unspoken connection sparking between them. Heather swallowed hard, mesmerized by Giles's gaze.

He leaned in, his voice taking on a slightly huskier tone. "Weren't you just telling me I need to be more experimental?"

Giles held out his hand, an unspoken invitation in his eyes. "As I tried the marshmallow peppermint concoction, it's your turn to have a dance with me."

Heather couldn't resist the magnetic pull, and her hand instinctively reached out to meet Giles's. Her heart raced as he warmly clasped her hand, and she felt a rush of exhilaration. Giles gently guided her to her feet and led her to the small dance floor. His arm circled her waist, their bodies moving harmoniously with the music. Heather, her free hand resting on his arm, was drawn closer to him. She rested her head against Giles's chest, the rhythm of their hearts uniting as one dance bled into a few others.

All too soon, the early morning hours signaled their departure. They had spoken and danced the night away, making the evening feel like a brief but magical interlude. As they strolled back to the hotel, Giles reached for Heather's hand, and they moved through the crisp morning air, enveloped in the enchanting hush of the early hours. The soft, romantic glow of the streetlights illuminated their path as they walked together in comfortable silence, each lost in their thoughts about the unexpectedly enjoyable evening they'd just shared.

Upon reaching the floor where their rooms were, Giles escorted Heather to her suite's door. She turned to bid him goodnight, only to be met with a heart-stopping kiss, sealing the evening with a powerful, unspoken connection. At that moment, Heather knew that serendipity had played a significant role in their encounter—not just once, but three times over.

CHAPTER SIX

G iles found himself on the way to Centennial Airport after an early morning conference call with a friend at the California Attorney General's office. Heather's revelation about the foundation had set his investigative gears in motion. He didn't waste any time that morning, immediately reaching out to his legal department for a list of all the foundations his company had ties to.

As he'd suspected, the Wildlife Guardians Foundation was not one of them. After ordering a single red rose with an attached invitation for Heather, he called his friend, Liam Shields, at the California Attorney General's Office, providing him with all the details he had. There was a promise to send more information once Heather handed over the documents she possessed.

Giles couldn't stand the fact that a fraudulent foundation had tarnished his company's reputation. He also couldn't bear the thought of people and animals being harmed, and he felt Heather's gaze weighing on his conscience. He had assured her he'd get to the bottom of the situation and fully intended to do so. If there were a chance to salvage the project afterward, Giles would make it happen.

Thoughts of Heather swept over him, causing his heart to quicken. Giles had never met anyone quite like her—magnificent and alluring. He knew he was falling for her. They were nearing the airport when his phone bleeped, and he couldn't help but smile when he saw a message from Heather.

If I agree to go to the dance with you, you have to agree to do something you're not comfortable with.

Giles laughed at Heather's witty response to his invitation to the Mistletoe Lodge Winter Festival Ball.

Deal! he typed back as the town car glided to the hangar where his helicopter awaited. Exiting the car, he was met by his long-standing pilot, Todd Spears.

"Hi, Todd," Giles greeted him.

"Hey, Giles," Todd responded in a barely audible voice, sneezing just after.

"Bless you," Heather's voice reached Giles as he saw her and Priscilla walking toward them. Another driver from the hotel was rushing after them with their luggage.

"Hello," Giles greeted them with a warm smile.

"Good morning, Giles," Priscilla was the first to greet him, followed by Heather. "What a lovely helicopter," she admired the aircraft.

"Thank you," Giles said, stepping aside for one of the airport staff to help Priscilla into the helicopter. He cast a concerned look at Todd, who seemed unwell. "Are you okay, Todd?" Giles inquired.

"I think I'm coming down with the flu," Todd confessed.

"Are you well enough to fly?" Giles questioned further.

"I'm fine," Todd assured him. "You did say there's a large enough shed to house the bird at Mistletoe Lodge, right?"

"Yes, there is," Heather said, introducing herself to Todd. "Hi, I'm Heather."

"Todd," he nodded. "Sorry, I can't shake your hand. I don't want to spread any germs I may have."

"I understand," Heather replied. "Are you sure you're well enough to fly?"

"I've got a bit of a headache, but it's not a long flight, so I should be okay," Todd said as he took the checklist from one of the hangar staff. "My grandparents live in Breckenridge, and I'm visiting them until I'm needed to fly again. I'll get a cab there and go straight to bed." He grinned. "I'm sure my grandmother will make sure I have lots of chicken soup to help me get better."

"Oh, that's nice," Heather responded with a warm smile before she turned to Giles, mentioning the Sikorsky S-76B. "It's a nice helicopter."

"Yes, it's been customized to meet Giles's specifications," Todd shared.

"Complete with the gold Holland Corporation emblem," Heather observed as she boarded.

"You know your helicopters," Giles remarked as he sat across from Heather and Priscilla.

"I've flown in a few," Heather shrugged. "But not as fancy as this one."

"The ones Heather has flown in are usually used for rescue missions," Priscilla elaborated.

"Of course," Giles acknowledged as he fastened his seatbelt, and the helicopter roared to life.

The flight conditions remained favorable, and within an hour, they began their descent, landing near a spacious barn that had once housed a small airplane owned by Mistletoe Lodge. As they disembarked from the helicopter, Giles couldn't help but be captivated by the breathtaking scenery. Towering woods enveloped the lodge, and the majestic Tenmile mountain range stood proudly in the distance, draped in a pristine white coat of snow.

Upon stepping onto the mountain soil, Giles inhaled the refreshing mountain air. Despite the distant sounds of the winter fair unfolding on the lodge's grounds, an undeniable tranquility and peace wrapped around the place, creating a serene contrast to the bustling festivities in the distance.

With excitement and anticipation, Giles and Todd assisted Priscilla in retrieving her luggage from the helicopter's storage while Heather deftly handled her bags. Together, they made their way toward Mistletoe Lodge. Giles was looking forward to seeing Avery and being shown around the lodge, and he'd finally get to meet the man who had broken his best friend's heart twelve years ago.

Giles was impressed by the sprawling lodge. It was much bigger than he'd anticipated and surprisingly modern when they entered the foyer. They put their luggage down by the entrance, and Todd was about to order a cab, but Priscilla got the concierge to order their town car to take Todd to Breckenridge. Todd said his goodbyes and went to wait for the town car.

"Rita, where is my grandson?" Priscilla asked the woman at the front desk.

"Ryder and Emily are in the back office," Rita told her, lowering her voice slightly. "I don't think now is a good time to go there. The situation is rather tense."

Pricilla sighed and shook her head before ignoring Rita's

warning and stalking toward the back office, beckoning Giles and Heather to follow her. As they neared the office, they could hear raised voices. Without knocking, Priscilla pushed the door open, startling the man and woman staring heatedly at each other. Priscilla pulled Giles inside before either of them could respond to the abrupt interruption, and Heather followed behind him.

"Ryder, Emily, I'd like you to meet Giles Holland." Priscilla introduced Giles to her grandchildren and the current owners of the lodge. "He's our guest who'll be staying in cabin number five."

Ryder nodded in acknowledgment, shaking Giles's hand. Anger still resonated in Ryder's eyes.

"Have either of you seen Avery?" Priscilla asked, her brows shooting up as Emily turned to her grandmother.

"Gran now's not a good time to bring up Avery," Emily told her, looking worriedly at Ryder.

"What's happened?" Priscilla asked, her accusing gaze turning on Ryder. "What did you do this time?"

"What did *I* do?" Ryder looked at his grandmother in disbelief.

Before he could say anything more, Emily cut him off by clearing her throat, and Giles saw her pointing her eyes toward him.

"I beg your pardon, Mr. Holland." Ryder picked up his phone and typed on it. "You must be tired after your trip from..."

"Los Angeles," Giles said, the first thing that popped into his brain. Heather was standing close beside him, and he found her presence distracting. He gave himself a mental shake. "And please, call me Giles."

Giles saw something that looked like recognition flash in Ryder's eyes.

"My brother-in-law, Hank, will be here in a few minutes with your luggage and to escort you to your cabin," Ryder informed him. "I don't want to be rude, but my sister and I have some pressing business to discuss with my grandmother."

"Of course," Giles said with a bow of his head.

Just as Giles was about to leave the office, a tall and instantly recognizable figure entered. It was none other than Hank Saunders, a renowned professional football player, and it dawned on Giles that this was the same Hank who would be showing him to his cabin.

"We'll meet for dinner and finalize everything," Priscilla told Giles.

Giles nodded in acknowledgment and followed Hank out of the office, wondering how Hank had ended up at Mistletoe Lodge.

"Can I take your luggage for you?" Hank asked him with a friendly smile.

"No, I can manage," Giles assured him, but Hank insisted on taking one of the bags. "You're Hank Saunders, the former Denver Broncos quarterback."

"Yeah, that's right." Hank nodded, adding, "I blew my knee out a couple of years ago and it ruined my football career."

"Do you work at Mistletoe Lodge?" Giles asked as they crunched through the snow.

"Yeah, I do," Hank told him. "I'm married to Emily, Ryder Carlisle's sister, so I'm invested in it."

That made sense. Giles nodded before he was suddenly captivated by the wooden cabins that came into view as they rounded what Giles could see were stables. As they walked toward one of the larger cabins, his gaze was caught by an orchard off to the side.

"Is that an orchard?" Giles asked, stopping to look at it.

"Yeah, it's Ryder's pet project now," Hank said. "He's growing mistletoe and apples." He started walking with Giles following him. "Ryder's and Emily's mother used to run the apple orchard. It was quite a lucrative business back then. Ryder and Emily have reopened the business."

"Oh, wow!" Giles said.

He was impressed by how hard the brother-sister duo had worked to restore Mistletoe Lodge to its former glory. That's when Giles knew he had made the right choice by investing in it.

Hank stopped before a large wooden cabin, number five, and opened the door. As they stepped inside, a rush of warm air enveloped Giles, carrying with it the welcoming scent of freshly cut pine and wood burning in the cozy fireplace of the living room. The cabin was spacious, with a rustic charm that blended seamlessly with modern comfort.

The living room featured a plush, oversized sofa and a stone hearth, where the fire crackled, casting a comforting glow throughout the room. Natural light streamed through large windows, revealing a breathtaking view of the snow-covered mountains in the distance. The wooden beams on the ceiling added to the cabin's rustic character, while the open kitchen was fully equipped with modern appliances. It was clear that every detail of the cabin was designed to provide guests with a warm and inviting retreat in the heart of the snowy wilderness.

"This is the main bedroom." Hank strolled down the hallway to the room at the end of it. "It has its own bathroom."

Hank put Giles's bag beside the door to highlight the room's features.

"You have two televisions with cable. One in here and the other in the living room." Hank pointed to the bedside table. "The remote for the television is in that drawer." He nodded pointedly at the bathroom. "The bathroom is through that door, and the balcony through those double doors links with the living rooms for a view of Tenmile."

"This is great," Giles said, looking around. "Thank you, Hank."

"Priscilla had us stock up the kitchen with the list sent by your assistant." Hank walked back toward the front door with Giles following him. "If you need anything, please call the front desk. A phone is on the wall near the kitchen and in your bedroom." He paused and said, "Oh, there is Wi-Fi as well."

A few minutes after Hank had left, Giles changed into more casual attire: jeans, a turtleneck shirt, and boots. He set up his laptop at the dining table. As he was getting settled, his phone rang. He glanced at the caller ID and saw that it was Liam Shields.

"Hi, Liam," Giles answered.

"Hey, Giles," Liam greeted. "I've got some news for you about that foundation—or at least the man who set up the foundation."

"So soon?" Giles was surprised.

"Yeah, as soon as I ran a search on the database for Gordon Jackson, it raised some major red flags," Liam explained. "And the next thing I knew, the FBI got involved."

"Oh?" Giles furrowed his brow, concern creeping in.

"It turns out Gordon Jackson is well-known by the FBI for using various charitable organizations for money laundering,"

Liam's words sent a shiver down Giles's spine. "I'm sorry, but they want to talk to you because I had to explain why I was looking into this guy."

"That's fine," Giles assured him.

He let out a deep breath, his face reflecting a mix of anxiety and frustration. This was not good at all. While Giles's company had always maintained a clean record and had nothing to hide, the involvement of Gordon Jackson and the FBI's interest could potentially lead to a full-scale investigation into his business operations. It wasn't just about clearing his name but also about safeguarding the reputation and integrity of his company.

If there was any wrongdoing or suspicious activity even remotely linked to his organization, it could spell trouble for his employees, shareholders, and the entire business he had worked so hard to build. The consequences were enormous, and Giles realized that he needed to get to the bottom of this situation quickly.

"I gave an agent your number. I hope that's okay?" Liam told him. "He'll be in contact soon."

"Okay." Giles nodded. "Do you know the name of the agent?"

Liam told him the agent's name. "If you need any advice or legal help, call any time of the day or night. Keep me updated on what's going on, and please still send those documents on the foundation through to me when you get them."

"I will do," Giles promised before ending the call.

Giles sat back, staring at his phone he'd just thrown onto the table. His mind reeling with the information Liam had just given him as another disturbing thought hit him. He may never have known about this foundation using his company's name if he'd never met Heather.

Giles picked up his phone and called Barb.

"Hello, Giles!" Barb's voice resonated with her annoyance at being disturbed on her vacation. "What's wrong?"

"I haven't even said hello, and you're asking what's wrong." Giles laughed.

"You only ever call after hours, on my days off, or during my vacation time if there's something wrong," Barb pointed out.

"I'm sorry to trouble you on your vacation, Barb." Giles propped the phone between his ear and shoulder so he could use his laptop at the same time. "And yes, I do need your help."

"Would it matter if I told you I'm in the Bahamas and don't have access to a laptop?" Barb drawled.

"Are you?" Giles frowned.

"Sure, let's go with that, put a pin in your problem, and address it after the festive season," Barb suggested.

"Mommy, can Sly come play?" Giles heard Oscar call in the background.

"Ah, so you're not in the Bahamas." Giles opened his email and started to type a letter to Barb. "As I recall, Sly is Oscar's friend who lives next door to you."

"There could be another Sly in the Bahamas," Barb tried her best to stop Giles from disturbing her vacation.

"What if you help with this urgent problem, and I promise to send you and Oscar to the Bahamas for a summer vacation next year—all expenses paid at a resort of your choice," Giles bargained.

"First-class all the way?" Barb asked.

"First-class all the way," Giles promised.

"Fine, what do you need from me?" Barb sighed resignedly.

Giles explained the situation with the fraudulent foundation. He wanted Barb to look into the African Wildlife and Rural Village Preservation Group that Heather had been working with on the African project. While Giles was now confident his organization had nothing to do with the fraudulent foundation, he still felt responsible for the failed project.

"You should've opened with this," Barb told him. "You know how passionate I am about conservation work like this." He didn't have to see her to see her smug smile. "It wouldn't have cost you a first-class trip to the Bahamas."

"If you can help me find out about the project and if there is anything we can do to restart it, it will be well worth sending you to the Bahamas." Giles finished typing the information he could remember from Heather's conversation. "I'll have more information about it in the next couple of days from the person who brought the fraudulent foundation to my attention."

"Who was that?" Barb asked him. "If I can get their name, it would help."

"Heather," Giles said, frowning, realizing he didn't know her last name.

"Well, that narrows it down to a couple of million people!" Barb said, sarcasm dripping off her tongue. "I'm going to need more than Heather."

"Would it help if I told you she's Priscilla Carlisle from Venter and Associates granddaughter?" Giles asked.

"No way!" Barb spluttered. "Fiery haired, green eyes, beautiful, outspoken..."

"Yes, that's her," Giles said.

"Jessop," Barb told him. "Her name is Heather Jessop."

"Do you know her?" Giles asked curiously.

"Do you watch Animal Planet?" Barb enquired.

"No, I can't say I do," Giles admitted.

"Then you should," Barb said. "Heather is on it quite often. She's one of the leading wildlife veterinarians."

"Seriously?" Giles's eyes widened in surprise. "I mean, I knew what she does for a living, and yes, she's incredible, but I didn't know she was so well known."

"That's if you watch Animal Planet or read animal magazines." Barb paused for a while.

The few seconds of silence felt like minutes. Giles thought she'd hung up.

"Barb?" Giles took his phone in his hands. "Are you still there?"

"You've met Heather Jessop?" Barb's voice was full of curiosity.

"Yes, we met yesterday and had dinner together," Giles answered honestly.

"There it is again!" Barb said.

"What?" Giles was confused.

"That catch in your voice whenever you mention Heather Jessop." Barb's voice had a hint of surprise in it. "You like her."

"What's not to like?" Giles tried to sound indifferent. "The woman is incredible."

"You've used incredible to describe her twice now." Barb laughed.

"Well, she is," Giles said, moving the conversation away from Heather. "Can we get back to the project?"

"Sure," Barb agreed. "Send me all the details, and I'll get to it first thing tomorrow morning. I'm taking Oscar and Sly ice skating."

"Enjoy," Giles told her, and an idea hit him. "How would you feel about a trip to Frisco for Christmas?"

"I can see where this is going." Barb sighed. "I take it Heather Jessop is at Mistletoe Lodge?"

"Yes, she is, and this project meant a lot to her," Giles explained. "She lost some good people when the project was abruptly terminated."

"You want me to come out there and entice Heather to head up the project," Barb guessed.

"This is why we work so well as a team, Barb," Giles teased. "You can read my mind."

"Fine," Barb relented. "But it will have to be the day after Christmas as we've already got plans for Christmas day."

"Deal," Giles agreed. "Make all the arrangements, and I'll get you a cabin here at the lodge."

Time flew by as Giles worked until a knock at his door distracted him. Before he opened it, he knew it was Heather. His heart started to pound in his chest, and Giles took a calming breath before opening the door. When he opened it, his breath caught in his throat when he saw her standing, smiling at him. Her cheeks were flushed from the cold. A woolen cap warmed her fiery hair. Matching mittens covered her hands, and the scarf around her neck completed the set. She was bundled into a puffy jacket that hung down her jean-clad legs, and fur-topped boots covered her feet.

"Hi!" Heather waved a mittened hand.

"Hi!" Giles said back. "You look cozy." He wanted to hit himself in the head for his stupid comment.

"Compliments of my grandmother!" Heather rolled her eyes. "You know the saying when a mother feels cold, the child gets bundled up. Well, that's my gran for you." She sighed. "Speaking of which, she's requested your presence at the lodge."

"Oh, is that the time already?" Giles's eyes widened in disbelief when he saw how late it was.

"We're having dinner around the open fire pit tonight," Heather told him. "And you're invited to join us." She pulled a sheepish face. "And we need your help with a mission."

"Oh, I thought your grandmother wanted to go over a few details of the investment for the lodge?" Giles frowned as the rest of her sentence sank in. "What mission?"

"My grandmother will fill you in, and then you're invited to dine with the younger generation once you have the mission plans." Heather grinned. "My grandmother doesn't enjoy sitting around the fire pit during the winter. She moans that it gets to her joints. And we all have to be up early tomorrow, so she needs to get to bed a lot earlier than us."

"Well, thank you. I'd love to join you for dinner," Giles told her, then realized he hadn't invited her in. "Sorry, come inside."

He stepped back, and Heather brushed past him, making him catch his breath again as her scent tantalized his senses. Giles had to force himself not to reach out and pull her to him. She walked into the living room and turned toward him.

"You're going to need something warm to put on," Heather warned him. "It gets icy in the evenings."

"Noted," Giles said. "I'll grab my jacket, scarf, cap, and gloves."

He disappeared into his bedroom, quickly grabbing the items, before rejoining her in the living room.

"Would you like something to drink?" Giles offered, noting she hadn't taken off her coat.

"No thanks," Heather declined. "My grandmother is waiting for you, and I want to sneak in a few smores before dinner."

"I'm beginning to notice you have a sweet tooth." Giles grinned as he donned his coat, scarf, gloves, and woolen cap.

"I do!" Heather nodded. "Much to my grandmother's disapproval and if you hear her speak about it—large dentist bills of mine."

Giles held the cabin door ajar, inviting Heather to step outside and embrace the breathtaking twilight. The snow had already cast a soft, glistening blanket over the landscape as the sun dipped below the horizon. Together, they strolled back to the lodge, their path illuminated by the soft glow of the moonlight.

As they walked, Heather shared stories of the quaint cabins, the newly cultivated orchard, and the mysteries of the surrounding forest. The air was crisp, and the silence magical. Nature whispered secrets to them and they listened with their hearts.

Near the stables, an unexpected visitor emerged. A swift and graceful snowshoe hare darted before them, its snowy fur blending seamlessly with the winter landscape. Startled by the unexpected guest, Heather tried to avoid a collision. However, her footing betrayed her, and with an endearing mix of grace and clumsiness, she tumbled into Giles, sending them both into the pristine snow.

Heather was nestled on top of Giles and the world seemed to hush around them. Their laughter faded, and in the serene stillness, their eyes locked. Heather's emerald gaze shimmered with concern, mirroring the infinite starlit sky above.

"Are you all right?" she asked in a tender whisper.

Giles, his breath visible in the chilly night air, struggled to regain his composure. "I'll survive," he replied with a playful wheeze.

Just as Heather was about to rise, their eyes locked, and time seemed to pause. Their mingling breaths danced in the frigid air, and an irresistible force drew their lips together. Giles wrapped his arms around her, and in that timeless moment, their kiss encapsulated the enchantment of the night, erasing the world around them.

CHAPTER SEVEN

A noise from the stables abruptly pulled Heather and Giles apart, and she heard her name being called in the distance. Startled, Heather sprang to her feet, her movements so swift that she almost lost her balance. Beside her, Giles stood, and she could see a flicker of uncertainty in his eyes.

"It's Emily," Heather said, her voice reflecting the urgency she felt, before she hurried off in the direction of her cousin's voice.

Heather's mind was still reeling from the lingering kiss they'd just shared. It was the second time their lips had met, and it had the same dizzying effect as the first, turning her thoughts into a delightful, swirling chaos.

Heather didn't look back to see if Giles was following her as she met Emily walking toward her.

"Did you fall?" Emily's shrewd eyes took in Heather's disheveled appearance. "You've got snow all over your wooly hat." She grinned. "Which you look so cute in."

"Seriously!" Heather glared at Emily. "I'm going to have static hair from this thing."

"Now, now, Heather. Gran's good friend Mrs. Timmins knitted that for you." Emily pursed her lips, trying not to laugh as she flicked snow and some leaves from Heather's hat and coat. "In emerald green to match your pretty eyes."

"You're really enjoying this, aren't you?" Heather's eyes narrowed.

"A little bit." Emily nodded. "Ryder and I had to endure Mrs. Timmins knitting every Christmas for most of our lives." She gave Heather a smug smile. "You used to get away with it because you lived in sunny California."

"She knitted me creepy woolen dolls!" Heather shuddered. "I have a trunk load of them shoved in my attic, and I swear at night I can hear their little wooly feet sliding over the floor at night as they have a wooly doll dance."

"I think the hat, scarf, and mittens are adorable." Giles's voice came from behind Heather, making her jump.

Emily tilted her head to look past Heather. "Goodness, Giles, did you fall in the snow too?"

"A rabbit jumped at me, and I tried to move out of its way and plowed into Giles," Heather explained in a rush, feeling her cheeks heat.

"Ah!" Emily nodded, looking apologetically at Giles. "I'm sorry you had to experience the Heather wrecking ball. She dislikes bunnies, and Heather will plow anyone down to escape them."

"You're afraid of bunnies?" Giles gaped at her in disbelief. "You get up close and personal with polar bears but are afraid of bunnies?"

"Yup!" Emily's grin was back as she nodded.

"I'm not afraid of bunnies!" Heather exclaimed and couldn't suppress a shudder. "They're just vicious."

"Vicious?" Giles was now looking at her, stunned. "Compared to polar bears?"

"Will you stop with the polar bears!" Heather glared at him and swung back toward her cousin. "And I'm not afraid of bunnies!" She looked at Giles once again. "Isn't my grandmother waiting for you?"

"Oh, yes, right!" Amusement flashed in Giles's eyes as he excused himself and went to find Priscilla inside the lodge.

"Thanks a lot, cuz!" Heather hissed at Emily. "Not only do I look like a creepy woolen doll, but now Giles thinks I'm afraid of bunnies."

"You don't look like a creepy woolen dolly!" Emily teased, linking arms with Heather. "You look like a cozy woolen dolly." Emily burst out laughing.

"You know I'm going to retaliate for this, right?" Heather warned Emily.

"I'm sure you will," Emily noted, tenderly squeezing Heather's arm. "But it was well worth it." She gave Heather a tight smile. "But I think we're even though."

"How do you figure that?" Heather looked at Emily, surprised.

"You come here all cool and exciting, making me number two on Rosie's cool relations list," Emily explained.

"This is payback for me being cool?" Heather looked at Emily with raised eyebrows.

"Yes," Emily confirmed with a nod, indicating Heather's outfit with her hand. "This makes you look less cool, and the fact that you're scared of bunnies."

"I'm *not* scared of bunnies!" Heather said, exasperated, although there was some truth in that.

"Yes, you are!" Emily persisted.

They walked toward the fire pits nestled at the rear of the lodge, the comforting glow of dancing flames guiding their way. The night sky stretched above, a velvet canvas adorned with a brilliant array of stars, casting their radiant twinkle over the majestic mountain range that towered in the background. The distant snow-packed peaks seemed to caress the heavens. Their silhouettes etched with elegance.

As they approached, the enticing aroma of barbecue wafted from one side, where seasoned grill masters were busy preparing a mouthwatering feast. The sizzle of cooking meat sent an eager tremor through her stomach, reminding her just how hungry she had become.

Emily expertly guided them to a prime spot reserved by Hank, a glowing fire pit inviting them to partake in its warmth. Hank had thoughtfully arranged a selection of delectable s'mores ingredients on a small table beside him, teasing their senses with the promise of sweet indulgence.

"The food smells wonderful," Heather grumbled. "I'm starving."

"Well, you're going to have to wait for our visitor," Emily told her, sitting beside Hank, who kissed her. "I see you got our prime fire pit seats, my darling."

"Only the best for my wife." Hank laughed, putting his arm around Emily's shoulders.

Heather stood watching them for a few seconds with a smile. She loved how in love Emily and Hank were. They were the ideal couple and a good role model for any marriage.

Heather sat opposite them and pulled off the stifling mitten with her teeth, sighing in relief when her hands were finally free from their wooly prison. She warmed her hands over the fire.

"So, what are the plans for our trip to Denver tomorrow?" Heather asked Emily and Hank.

"Well, Ryder called to let us know that he's found Avery and that if she forgives him, he's going to propose." Emily's eyes shone happily as she cuddled closer to Hank.

"I'm glad they found their way back to each other," Hank said, picking up graham crackers, marshmallows, and some shavings of chocolate. He squished them together, put them on a s'mores stick, and held it over the fire. "I hope Avery forgives him and accepts Ryder's proposal."

"You're such a softy." Emily sighed and put her head on Hank's shoulder as he moved the stick toward Heather when the s'more was ready. "There you go, that should fill a little gap until dinner."

"Thank you, Hank," Heather said, taking the gooey treat from the stick. "You're my hero."

"You're welcome," Hank said with a big grin. "Do you want one?" He looked questioningly at Emily.

"No, thank you." Emily shook her head and turned to Heather. "If Avery accepts his proposal, Gran wants us up at the crack of dawn to run errands."

"I know," Heather assured Emily as she ate the delicious s'more. "We have to set up a surprise engagement party for when they return to Mistletoe tomorrow."

"Did you ask Giles if he'd be willing to use his helicopter to get them from Denver?" Emily looked at Heather.

"No, Gran said she was going to." Heather licked the stickiness from her fingers.

"Speaking about Giles..." Emily raised an eyebrow as she

looked at Heather. "Gran tells me that you and he are getting along *well*."

"Yes, we are," Heather admitted. "I've agreed to be his date to the Winter Festival Ball tomorrow night."

"Wow!" Hank and Emily said in unison.

"You must really like him to agree to go to a formal event!" Emily's eyes widened. But there was no teasing in her eyes, only concern. "Just be careful." Her voice dropped. "You don't want your heart broken again."

"Giles and I are just friends," Heather told them, not sure if she was trying to convince her cousin or herself of that. "I was not amused when I found out who he was." She smiled, remembering how she'd verbally attacked him about his company's part in what had happened in Africa. "His company's foundation was responsible for the clean water project in Africa."

"No!" Emily hissed in surprise. "The project where all those villagers and animals died because of that dam not being built correctly?"

"Yes." Heather nodded. "But Giles didn't have any recollection of the foundation. I believe he didn't, and he's going to investigate it."

"That's good," Hank said. "I remember how that project upset you."

"Yes, that's the year Hank and I went to Los Angeles to visit you when you returned from Africa," Emily reminded them. "You were so upset."

"I remember." The tall man walking out the back door caught Heather's attention. Her breath caught in her throat, her stomach fluttered, and her heart went wild. "There's Giles."

"Oh, good," Hank said. "I'm starved."

"I hope he's agreed to send his helicopter to get Avery and Ryder," Emily said, turning to watch Giles approach them.

"Hi," Giles greeted them, taking a seat beside Heather. "The barbeque smells delicious."

"We can eat as soon as you're ready," Emily told him.

"The sooner, the better," Hank added, amusement glinting in his eyes as he looked at Heather. "Heather and I will get hangry if we don't eat soon."

"Were you waiting for me?" Giles looked at them apologetically. "I'm sorry."

"If you send your helicopter to get Avery and Ryder from Denver, we'll forgive you!" Heather gave him an alluring smile.

"I've already agreed to that," Giles told them, laughing at Heather's request. "I've already messaged my pilot, and I'm waiting for him to respond to find out when he can be here tomorrow."

"Thank you!" Emily breathed a sigh of relief. "I suppose my grandmother filled you in on the surprise engagement party we want to throw Avery and Ryder tomorrow afternoon."

"She did," Giles confirmed. "It's going to be a big day tomorrow with the festival ending, their engagement party, and the Winter Festival Ball that evening."

"That's why we need your helicopter." Heather stood and led the way to the food.

They dished up some food and went back to the fire pit. The four of them made small talk as they ate, and after dinner, they had sherry while Hank made s'mores. The conversation had switched to the lodge and the plans Emily, Ryder, and Hank were implementing.

Heather was unashamedly on her fourth s'more when Priscilla dashed out the lodge's back door.

"Emily, Heather, I need your help," Priscilla called, rushing toward them.

"Gran!" Emily called, jumping up alongside Heather with Hank and Giles close behind them as they made their way to Priscilla. "Are you okay?"

Heather's heart was beating erratically as shock waves of fright coursed through her, wondering what had happened to her grandmother.

"Yes, I'm fine," Priscilla assured them with a frown. "I've been trying to call all of you." She held up her phone, showing them the unanswered calls.

"Oh, sorry, Gran," Emily answered. "We didn't hear our phones."

"What happened, Gran?" Heather's heart started to slow down.

"There's been a development with Ryder and Avery." Priscilla's eyes sparkled with excitement. "Avery said yes to Ryder's proposal." Her hand rubbed the bottom of her throat. "The plans for tomorrow have changed."

"Really?" Heather said, looking pained. "We've already painstakingly planned the engagement party."

"It's no longer an engagement party." Priscilla's smile spread slowly across her lips. "We're planning a wedding."

"What?" Heather, Emily, Hank, and Giles spluttered in unison.

"In a day?" Emily choked. "Gran, there's no way we can plan a wedding in a day."

"Not a day, Emily, sweetheart," Priscilla told him. "We have about six hours tomorrow morning to do it."

"Are you sure you didn't hit your head, Gran?" Heather

looked at her grandmother skeptically. "How on earth are you going to plan a wedding in six hours?"

"I've already started," Priscilla explained. "Ryder said that he and Avery are going to get married in court tomorrow after he's secured the marriage license."

"So…" Heather looked sideways at her gran with narrowed eyes. "The engagement party is now a wedding reception?"

"No, honey." Priscilla shook her head. "We're going to Denver to place the entire wedding at the bed and breakfast Avery is currently staying at."

"Are you sure you didn't hit your head?" It was Emily's turn to look at her grandmother as if she had a concussion. "You want us to plan and set everything up in Denver?"

"Yes." Priscilla nodded and looked at her phone as it bleeped a few times. "Oh good, Candice from the bridal boutique in Silverthorne will open for us at five tomorrow morning."

"Gran, you want us to get to Silverthorne by five?" Emily gaped at Priscilla as if she'd lost her mind.

"Has your pilot responded, Giles?" Priscilla ignored Emily's question and turned to Giles.

"I'll check." Giles pulled out his phone and checked. "Yes, and unfortunately, we don't have a pilot. Todd is sick."

"Would you be open to another pilot flying your aircraft?" Priscilla asked Giles.

"As long as they are experienced and licensed." Giles nodded. "I don't see a problem."

"Hank, what about your father?" Priscilla looked at him.

"My father doesn't fly anymore since he had that eye operation," Hank told her, looking apologetic. "But I can ask if he knows another pilot."

"Hang on!" Heather interrupted and held up her hand. "I know a pilot." Hank raised an eyebrow and smiled. Heather narrowed her eyes warningly at him. "They are experienced and licensed."

"Has this pilot flown a helicopter all over the world in the most extreme weather and got most of their flying experience volunteering for sea rescue with the Coast Guard?" Hank asked.

"Yes, Hank, *they* have!" Heather looked at him challengingly.

"I thought *that* pilot didn't fly *locally*," Hank said cryptically.

"I guess things change," Heather told him.

"It's about time!" Hank gave her an impressed look.

"What are you two talking about?" Emily looked at the two of them suspiciously.

"Do you know the pilot Heather has in mind, Hank?" Giles asked him.

"I do," Hank confirmed. He glanced at Heather.

"Are they good enough to fly that beautiful helicopter of Giles's?" Pricilla asked Hank.

"They are," Hank told them, looking at Heather again. "They are one of the best helicopter pilots, and that comes from my father."

"Your father flies helicopters?" Giles asked Hank.

"He used to fly for the Marines," Hank told Giles proudly. "When he retired, he opened up a flying school." He smiled. "The pilot Heather and I are talking about was one of my father's first students."

"That's good," Giles said with a nod and looked at Heather. "Do you think they would be available at such short notice?"

"I'm sure," Heather said with certainty, then moved on to another subject. "Gran, how are we going to get to Silverthorne and back then to Denver in time to set up a wedding."

"There's a helipad on top of the mall," Priscilla told them and looked at Heather. "This pilot of yours needs to be here and ready by the time we leave." She looked at Emily. "Would you know what wedding dress Avery would like?"

"Actually, I do," Emily replied. "We looked at it when we were in Silverthorne earlier today to get our ball gowns." She looked at Heather. "Speaking of ball gowns, what are you going to wear tomorrow night?"

"Gran picked something out for me," Heather answered, suddenly realizing she hadn't seen it yet, then pushed it to the back of her mind. "Are we going to make up Avery's wedding party?" Emily nodded. "What are we going to wear?"

"You and Emily can come with me, and we can go through the boutique's website," Priscilla told Heather and Emily before turning to Hank and Giles. "What are the two of you going to wear?"

"I have a few suits," Giles told her and looked at Hank.

"I have a few as well," Hank answered.

"Good, that's you two sorted." She rubbed her chin. "We'll have to find a flower girl dress for Rosie and find out what Avery's parents are going to wear."

"Speaking of Avery's parents," Emily said. "Has anyone told them what's happening?"

"I did." Priscilla flipped through the messages, blipping on her phone. "Avery's mother has just confirmed her friend, a Denver judge, is available tomorrow." She smiled. "And the judge will help Ryder with the wedding license."

"Wow, Gran!" Heather gave a low whistle. "You've managed to organize this in a few hours."

"Forty minutes," Priscilla corrected her absently. She looked at them. "May Partridge, who owns May's Cottage Bed and

Breakfast where Avery is staying, is on board. She'll cater for our small party and have a cake ready."

"Geez, Gran!" Heather laughed. "You should open a wedding in a box business to help people plan spur-of-the-moment weddings."

Priscilla glanced up from her phone and blinked at Heather. "That's such a good idea for a business."

"It is," Giles agreed and smiled at Heather, making the butterflies in her stomach go wild as her heart thudded erratically.

She quickly looked away, feeling weak-kneed.

Pricilla checked the time on her phone. "Goodness, it's late." She looked at the four people staring at her in awe. "Are the four of you done eating?"

"We are," Hank answered.

"Then I suggest we get to bed as we have to be up in a couple of hours if we're going to pull this off," Priscilla suggested. "And one more thing. Avery doesn't know we're planning a surprise wedding for her. She thinks she and Ryder are getting married in court."

"Wow, Gran!" Heather looked at her, impressed. "Not only have you managed to organize an entire wedding in a flash, but a surprise one to boot."

"Honey, I've pulled together much bigger functions with far less and under more pressure," Priscilla assured her. "Now come along, you two." She indicated toward Emily and Heather. "You have to come pick out dresses so Marta can have them ready."

"How's she going to know our sizes?" Heather grinned at the exasperated look her grandmother shot her.

"Say goodnight, and meet me at my cottage." With that,

Priscilla said goodnight to Hank and Giles, thanking him for his help.

"Well, I guess this ends our evening," Heather sighed and turned to look at Giles. "Do you know your way back to your cabin?"

"I'm sure I'll manage," Giles smiled, and he seemed as hesitant to say goodnight as she was. "I guess I'll see you all in the morning."

With that, he said goodnight and walked off into the night. Heather's heart sank as she watched him leave. But her melancholy thoughts were interrupted when Emily gathered her things and Hank approached Heather.

"You know your grandmother isn't going to be happy when she sees the pilot you have in mind?" Hank warned her. "You should've told her."

"What?" Heather grinned sheepishly. "And spoil the surprise?" Her grin grew. "At least now she and the rest of my family will know."

"I think they already know what a rebel you are!" Hank laughed before turning his attention to Emily. "I'll see you at home when you're done with your Gran."

Emily nodded and kissed him before she and Heather went to Priscilla's cottage.

"So, who is this mystery pilot?" Emily looked at Heather suspiciously. "Please don't tell me it's Rand Myers?"

"What's wrong with Rand Myers?" Heather asked.

"Honey, if it's Rand, Hank's right in saying Gran isn't going to be happy," Emily warned her. "He broke your heart."

"That was years ago," Heather reminded Emily. "Rand and I have moved on. We've put our differences behind us."

"Well, Gran hasn't," Emily informed her. "She still doesn't greet the man if we bump into him in Frisco."

"Gran has to get over that." Heather sighed. "Our break up wasn't all Rand's fault. We wanted different things."

"Okay!" Emily held up her hands in surrender. "The thing is, Rand moved on, but what about you, Heather?" Her eyes filled with concern. "It's been four years since you and he ended your engagement, and you haven't even looked at anyone else, let alone dated."

"I haven't had time, Em." Heather gave her a reassuring smile. "I promise my heart healed over Rand a long time ago. I've just been incredibly busy with all the projects I've been working on."

"Gran thinks you buried yourself in your work to hide from your heartache." Emily squeezed Heather's arm.

"Gran's wrong," Heather assured Emily. "Now, we'd better get inside before Gran storms out here."

The cousins spent the next hour finding dresses for the next day, and by the time Emily went home, most of the wedding had been planned. Heather fell into bed after a hot shower and hid the matching wooly scarf, cap, and mittens. Her mind was racing with everything that had happened in the past two days and all that needed to be done the next day. Finally, she drifted to sleep to the images of hers and Giles kissing in the snow.

CHAPTER EIGHT

Giles arose early the following morning, eager to prepare for their journey. Hank's father, David, had arrived to assist in readying the helicopter, ensuring everything was meticulously fueled and inspected. Priscilla, Rosie, and Emily entered just as they wrapped up their preparations. Giles turned, heart pounding with anticipation, but was somewhat disheartened when Heather didn't appear alongside them.

"Good morning," Priscilla warmly greeted, her gratitude directed at David. "Thank you for all your help, David."

"Not a problem at all," David replied, "I've checked the weather conditions, and they're looking favorable. You're clear for a landing at Centennial Airport in Denver."

"Great news," Giles acknowledged. "What about the mall?"

"Everything's been cleared for that, too," David reassured him, casting a curious gaze around. "Where's the pilot?"

"On the way," Hank responded as they waited.

"Ah, there's Heather now," Priscilla joyfully exclaimed,

causing Giles's heart to skip a beat. "I wonder where her pilot friend is?"

Giles watched in awe as Heather approached, her fiery hair cascading over her shoulders. She exuded confidence, wearing a black t-shirt peeking from beneath her bomber jacket. Her denim-clad legs met her favorite boots, a backpack hung casually over one shoulder, and a pair of aviators dangled from her hand. Giles watched as time seemed to slow down, his senses absorbed by this captivating sight.

"Good morning, Gran," Heather greeted, her voice warm and cheerful. "Hello, David," she added, acknowledging Hank's father with a fond smile. "Is the bird ready?"

"Yes, she's all set," David affirmed. "A real beauty, too."

Heather agreed with a nod and accepted the clipboard handed to her. With precision, she reviewed the log, signing it with confidence before handing it back to David.

"Um, Heather, where's the pilot?" Giles inquired, confusion etched across his face as he observed Heather, then glanced at his wristwatch. "We're running a bit behind schedule."

"Yes, where is this pilot friend of yours, Heather?" Priscillas asked as she surveyed the grounds in bewilderment, searching for the mystery pilot.

"I'm here!" Heather responded with a tight smile as she put her aviators on her head and turned toward the cockpit before anyone could react.

"Heather's the pilot!" Giles, Priscilla, and Emily exclaimed in disbelief, their eyes locked on the cockpit as they watched her skillfully swing into it, buckle up, and start fiddling with gadgets.

"You've got to be kidding, right?" Emily gawked at Hank. "She's joking, right?"

David leaned in and went over a few things with Heather as the rest of them came to terms with who would be flying them around in the helicopter for the day.

"Seriously?" Giles muttered, speechless, his gaze fixated on the cockpit. He turned to Hank. "Heather's the pilot she was talking about last night?"

"Indeed she is!" Hank confirmed.

"Don't fret, my boy," David closed the cockpit door and consoled Giles, patting his shoulder reassuringly. "Heather's an exceptional pilot, one of the finest. I assure you. She's handled her fair share of helicopters."

"Heather was the pilot who logged most of her flight hours working with the Coast Guard?" Giles inquired, still in shock, as he tried to wrap his mind around it.

"That's correct," David confirmed for Hank. "I've flown alongside her many times, and trust me, Heather's capable of managing the most challenging conditions."

"Heather!" Priscilla directed her message to the closed cockpit door, her tone both incredulous and furious. "This is far from over. We'll have a thorough discussion when we return to the lodge."

"I think we ought to board now," Hank suggested, ushering them onto the aircraft, bidding farewell to his father.

Giles climbed in after Priscilla, Emily, and Rosie. He fastened his seatbelt, his mind racing. "Is there anything Heather can't do?" he whispered to himself.

"Cook!" Emily chimed in. "Heather can't cook."

"No, she certainly can't!" Rosie, Ryder's nine-year-old daughter, chimed in, her face twisted in disgust, and she shuddered. "She burned the hot dogs."

Giles chuckled at the young girl's repulsion. It was difficult to fathom Heather's culinary shortcomings. As the helicopter roared to life, they took off, embarking on their impromptu journey to a wedding in Denver. As he observed the Carlisles and their extended family, Giles couldn't help but smile. These were remarkable people, and he was reminded once again that investing in the lodge had been one of the best decisions he'd ever made.

The helicopter touched down on the Silverthorne Mall's roof without so much as a bump. They waited for the blades to stop whirring before Hank slid the door open, and they exited the aircraft. They walked a safe distance away, waiting for Heather, who confidently jumped out of the cockpit and strode toward them as if it were just another day.

"I hope the trip was smooth," Heather teased them and was met with wide-eyed stares. "Okay, so I can fly a helicopter." She shrugged.

"How long have you been flying helicopters?" Priscilla hissed.

"About six years, give or take a year or two." Heather quickly turned and walked toward the entrance a mall cop was holding open for them. "Good morning." She cheerfully greeted the man before slipping past him.

Giles stood back for a few seconds, once again admiring Heather in awe.

"She's magnificent," Giles said under his breath, sighing because he knew he was no longer falling for Heather—he was head over heels in love with her.

Heather truly was one in a billion, and as he followed the family into the deserted shopping mall, he knew she was the one for him. As they walked to the wedding boutique, Giles made a mental note to put—*learn to fly a helicopter*—on his to-do list.

An hour later, they were on their way to Denver. Avery's parents, whom Giles hadn't seen since last Christmas, met them at the mall and were with them on the trip. Giles was thankful he'd bought the larger Airbus helicopter as he looked at the six people around him. Laughter and excitement buzzed through the cabin as everyone anticipated the long-awaited wedding between Avery and Ryder.

The morning went by in a blur of preparations and the wedding. Giles had a lump in his throat at how beautiful the ceremony was. Priscilla had done an excellent job with the quick wedding setup. Avery and Ryder were driving back to the lodge while the party with Giles flew with him to Mistletoe Lodge. Giles hadn't had much time to speak to Heather and couldn't wait for the ball later.

It was late afternoon when they arrived at the lodge. Priscilla went to rest for an hour while Emily and Hank took Rosie for ice cream. Once the helicopter was secured, David left the lodge. Giles had waited for Heather, and when she saw him leaning against the door of the airplane shed, she smiled.

"Hey," Heather greeted him as she walked toward him. "It's been quite a day, hasn't it?"

"Your family has the best vacations *ever*." Giles laughed, pushing himself away from the wall. "Is it always this way?"

"If you mean, is there always some sort of drama?" Heather started walking toward the lodge, and he followed. "Then yes." She stopped, and her eyes shone teasingly. "But this is the first year we've been able to play with a helicopter."

"Yes, about that!" Giles raised his brows.

"Don't remind me." Heather sighed. "My grandmother is *not* thrilled that I went behind her back and learned to fly."

"Why didn't she want you to learn to fly?" Giles asked.

"Do you want to get a hot chocolate from one of the booths before they finish?" Heather asked him, and he nodded as she led the way.

"Don't think I'll let you off answering the question." Giles and Heather dodged people rushing to get some last-minute shopping done.

"When I was eighteen, my grandfather had a light aircraft." Heather stopped at the booth she was looking for. "Two cocoas, please."

"Cocoa?" Giles looked at her, surprised. "I was expecting something loaded with chocolate and cream."

"I figured you've been such a good sport today. You deserved your plain old cocoa." Heather laughed. "And I thought I'd have one with you."

"Loaded with caramel syrup," Giles noted when the lady from the booth handed them their steamy cocoa.

"What can I say?" Heather shrugged. "I love icky sweet hot beverages."

They took their cocoa, and Heather led them to a bench at the forest's edge that looked down on the lodge and fair. It had a breathtaking view with an iced-over lake glinting in the distance.

"It's beautiful here," Giles murmured.

"It's one of my favorite spots." Heather sipped her sweet beverage.

"You were telling me about your flying lessons," Giles reminded her as he sipped his cocoa.

"My grandfather started to teach me how to fly his light

aircraft," Heather explained. "I love it." She grinned as she looked at him. "I wanted to be either a fight pilot or a wildlife veterinarian."

"Oh!" Giles looked surprised. "I'm glad you chose to be a vet."

"So was my Gran," Heather told him. "Especially when her older brother was killed in my grandfather's light aircraft."

"I'm sorry to hear that," Giles said, compassion resonating in his voice. "It makes sense now why your grandmother didn't want you to take your pilot's license."

"Which made no sense to me." Heather shook her head. "I mean, she flies all the time, and so do I. So what difference does it make if I'm a passenger or the pilot?"

"It's like someone who doesn't drive because they fear it but get chauffeured around instead." Giles shrugged. "Mind games."

"Exactly!" Heather shivered and hunched into her coat.

"You're cold!" Giles moved closer, and Heather snuggled in toward him. "Do you want my coat?"

"No." Heather declined. "I'm fine."

"What happened with your pilot's license?" Giles persisted.

"When Hank's father opened his helicopter training center, I wanted to learn to fly, but my Grandmother forbade it." Heather looked at her cup. "But I went anyway, and David was so kind he kept my secret. I volunteered with the Coast Guard while studying in Los Angeles."

"You flew rescue helicopters." Giles was impressed.

"I did." Heather nodded. "It was exhilarating."

"You not only brave wild animals but pit your wits against nature as well." Giles sighed and wrapped his arm around her to stop her from shivering. "You are truly one of a kind, Heather."

"Thank you." Heather's eyes narrowed and she looked at him. "I think."

"You kept the fact that you had your helicopter pilot license from your grandmother all this time." Giles shook his head.

"It wasn't hard." Heather shrugged. "I don't tell my family about my adventures." She sipped her cocoa. "They only know bits and pieces of what I tell them." She raised her eyebrows and pursed her lips. "Trust me, it would put my grandmother in an early grave if she knew everything about my work."

"I can imagine," Giles said. "Have you been married or engaged?"

"Engaged." Heather turned the cup in her hands. "But we ended it four years ago, and since then, I've been too busy for relationships." She glanced at him. "How about you?"

"I was engaged for two years, but it ended when she went away for a weekend with her ex-boyfriend," Giles told her, surprised at how he no longer felt angry about it.

"I'm sorry, Giles." Heather's eyes filled with compassion. "How long ago did you break things off?"

"A year ago." Giles looked out over the lake in the distance and the towering mountains as the afternoon slid into early evening.

"Do you want to talk about it?" Heather looked at him.

"It's okay," Giles smiled thankfully at her. "It was more a relief than anything else, as we weren't compatible."

"Ah, so she did you a favor then." Heather guessed.

"That's how I see it," Giles confirmed and looked at the scenery again. "It's like sitting in the middle of a postcard."

"I know." Heather nodded and looked toward the mountains. "When I was a little girl, I thought the mountains were guardians that looked out for the lodge."

"That's so sweet." Giles grinned at her.

His phone rang.

"Excuse me." Giles reluctantly pulled his arm away from around her shoulder and put his cocoa on the bench beside him as he answered his phone. "Hi, Liam."

"Hi, can you talk?" Liam asked.

"Can I call you back in ten minutes?" Giles asked.

"Sure," Liam answered. "I'm at the office for another half an hour."

"I just need ten minutes to get to my cabin," Giles assured him.

When he hung up, he turned and looked apologetically at Heather. "I'm sorry, but I must take this call at the cabin as its business."

"You go ahead," Heather told him. "I have to go face my grandmother and get ready for the ball."

"Does this mean you're my date for tonight?" Giles's heart started pounding as he waited for her confirmation.

"Yes." Heather nodded. "We can meet in the foyer of the grand lodge at seven-thirty."

"I'll be there." Giles stood, picked up his cocoa, and, on impulse, leaned down and kissed her. "Until tonight." His voice was husky as their eyes met.

"Until tonight." Heather's voice was soft and her eyes darkened with emotion.

Giles walked to his cabin as if he was walking on air. When he was sitting at the dining table with his laptop, he video-called Liam, who answered on the third ring.

"Hi," Giles greeted. "Sorry about that."

"Not a problem," Liam said. "Giles, I found out that the

foundation you asked me to look into that Gordon Jackson set up was affiliated with your company."

"What?" Giles's brow furrowed. "How?"

"I'm not sure yet," Liam told him. "I'm waiting for the registration documents."

"Thanks." Giles ran a hand through his hair. "How do you know it's affiliated with my corporation?"

"The FBI agent told me," Liam informed him. "When I looked into Gordon Jackson, I also looked for the foundation you mentioned. The FBI were on it like flies to sticky paper. They, too, were not aware of the foundation."

"If the FBI has Gordon Jackson in their sights, how would they not know about this foundation?" Giles was confused.

"The man's a whizz at hiding things," Liam explained. "They're trying to find over fifty million dollars unaccounted for."

"I hope they don't think I know the man or where to find him?" Giles said.

"The interesting thing is that Gordon Jackson is in prison," Liam shocked Giles by saying. "But the FBI is convinced he's still running his criminal enterprises on the outside."

"Awesome!" Giles blew out a breath. "Why target my company?" His frown deepened. "I don't even know the man."

"I'm not sure about that," Liam admitted. "But we'll find out once we've dug deeper into the foundation and him."

"Thanks, buddy," Giles was genuinely grateful that Liam had his back. "Any idea when the FBI will knock on my door?"

"No, sorry." Liam shook his head. "I'll try to find out."

After the call ended, Giles found a few messages from Barb. He called her.

"Where have you been?" Barb asked. "I was about to file a missing person report, as I've been trying to call you all day."

"I was at a wedding in Denver," Giles explained.

"Oh!" Barb exclaimed. "I've found out about that project in Africa."

"Great," Giles said, his interest piqued.

"The dam that was eventually built wasn't near the size it was supposed to be, and it's not built to a quality standard," Barb told him. "The locals have endless problems with it, and its water has been contaminated. The locals have to walk for miles for fresh water."

"I want to look into building it to the standards it should've been," Giles instructed. "After Christmas, would you be able to get the project started? I'll need you to come out to Frisco and meet Heather, as she'll be a valuable source of information."

"Sure." Barb agreed. "Now, if you don't mind, I'm going to spend some quality time with my son. Merry Christmas, Giles."

"Merry Christmas, Barb." Giles hung up and sat back in the chair, staring at the blank screen. "I have a feeling this is going to be a bumpy ride."

He looked at the large clock hanging over the kitchen door, and his eyes widened. It was time to get ready for the ball. Giles closed his laptop and went to have a shower.

An hour later, Giles was waiting in the foyer of the grand lodge.

"You always did clean up nicely," Avery's soft voice made him turn around to see her standing watching him.

"You look beautiful," Giles told her honestly.

Avery wore a strapless, ethereal, soft pink gown. The dress elegantly tapered at her waist, accentuating her natural curves.

Its delicate skirt cascaded gracefully down to her feet, and with every step, it seemed to waltz around her in a mesmerizing ballet. As she moved, a glimpse of matching pink pumps would occasionally peek out from beneath the gown's hem, adding a touch of subtle sophistication to her enchanting attire.

"I didn't get to thank you for helping with everything today," Avery said. "It meant the world to me."

"Of course." Giles smiled. "I'm just glad I got to be a part of your special day." He grinned. "Ashley's going to be mad that she missed it."

"And that I didn't wear one of her wedding dresses." Avery laughed. Her attention was caught when Ryder walked out from the back office.

"Hi," Ryder greeted Giles. "I wanted to thank you for today."

"Your wife already did." Giles shook Ryder's offered hand. "Congratulations, by the way."

"Thank you," Ryder said, his head turning toward his beautiful wife. "You look stunning, my love."

"Thank you." Avery gave a small curtsey and looked at Giles as she took Ryder's arm. "Where is your date for the dance?"

"Right here." Heather's voice made them all turn toward the door.

Giles stood in awe, his jaw dropping slightly as he beheld the breathtaking vision approaching them. She graced the scene in an emerald green mermaid silhouette dress that lovingly embraced her gentle, supple curves, and cascaded elegantly to the floor. A sultry slit ventured up the side of the dress, revealing her toned calf muscles as she elegantly sported two-inch, matching strappy heels that accentuated her shapely legs.

Giles couldn't help but gulp as his eyes indulged in the sumptuous sight before him. The dress featured a daring plunging neckline, its shoestring straps tastefully draping over her shoulders and accentuating the delicate contour of her collarbones. Her fiery hair, collected in a sweeping manner from her face, flowed down one shoulder in a cascade of luscious, flaming curls.

Her cleverly applied makeup showcased her high cheekbones and pert nose, while her striking green eyes sparkled beneath a curtain of thick, enchanting lashes. The entire ensemble rendered her an ethereal sight, a radiant embodiment of beauty and grace.

"Heather!" Avery breathed. "You look stunning."

Avery's voice broke the spell he'd fallen under upon seeing Heather.

"Thank you," Heather said with a smile. "You look just as stunning, Avery."

Once they exchanged compliments and pleasantries, Ryder and Avery excused themselves and left for the ball.

"I'm guessing you didn't rent that tux," Heather teased. She retrieved a matching emerald cape with a pristine white faux fur lining. As she was about to drape it over her shoulders, Giles gently intervened, taking the cloak from her.

"Allow me," Giles insisted, his voice carrying a hint of raspiness, which he quickly cleared as he enveloped Heather in the splendid cape—the intoxicating scent of fresh lilies intertwined with the moment. "You look like a princess," he declared, his words reverberating in the night air, a testament to Heather's radiant beauty.

"You don't have to be nice." Heather gave a nervous laugh. "My grandmother picked this outfit out for me."

"Your grandmother has exquisite taste," Giles remarked. "Shall we?" He put his coat on and offered her his arm.

"Let's." Heather put on a posh voice, and they walked out of the lodge toward the marquee where the Winter Festival Ball was being held.

Giles and Heather entered the Winter Festival Ball to a dazzling display of festive splendor. The marquee had been transformed into a winter wonderland, with glistening ice sculptures that seemed to defy gravity. Icicles adorned the ceilings, and crystal chandeliers dangled overhead, casting a whimsical glow across the room. A vast, frozen landscape had been recreated inside the marquee, complete with artificial snow, glistening evergreens, and snow-covered cottages, evoking a sense of being in a charming alpine village.

The guests were elegantly dressed, and the atmosphere was filled with laughter and joyous chatter. The tables were beautifully set with sparkling silverware and delicate china, adorned with white and silver centerpieces. The music of a live orchestra permeated the air, filling the space with enchanting melodies.

Walking deeper into the ballroom, they noticed a grand Christmas tree adorned with twinkling lights and ornaments that seemed to dance in the soft light. Couples swayed to the music on a spacious dance floor, their movements graceful and joyful. Giles couldn't help but admire the enchanting scene surrounding them and could sense Heather's fascination with the magical ambiance. The Winter Festival Ball was nothing short of spectacular, a dreamlike celebration of the season.

"It's gorgeous!" Heather exclaimed in awe.

"Your family has outdone themselves," Giles said as a hostess approached them.

"Welcome," the hostess smiled. "May I take your coats?"

"Thank you," Heather replied as Giles helped her with her cape, then took off his coat, handing them to the hostess.

"Heather, you and Giles are at the main table." The woman smiled, pointing to where the Carlisle family and friends were gathered.

They thanked her and made their way toward the table. Before they got there, a tall man with dark hair and amber eyes stopped them.

"Giles Holland?" The man asked.

"Yes." Giles nodded with a smile.

"Could I have a moment of your time?" The man gave Heather a tight smile. "I won't keep him long."

"No problem," Heather said, walking off.

"I'm sorry, but do I know you?" Giles frowned. The man did look vaguely familiar.

"I'm Zac Shields," Zac introduced himself.

"Shields?" Giles's frown deepened. "Are you related to Liam?"

"He's my older brother." Zac slightly lifted a corner of his tuxedo to reveal an FBI badge.

"You're the FBI agent." Giles nodded as annoyance spread through him. "You couldn't have waited until after Christmas?"

"Crime doesn't go away just because it's Christmas," Zac pointed out. "I thought I'd introduce myself to you and hoped we could meet at your cabin tomorrow afternoon?"

"Can't this wait until I'm back in Los Angeles?" Giles asked.

"I'm afraid not," Zac said. "We have reason to believe that Gordon Jackson has someone working in your corporation." He looked around the room. "Unless you're willing to watch the empire you've created crumble, the sooner we get ahead of this, the better."

"Fine. Can we meet at two tomorrow afternoon?" Giles felt icy fingers creep up his spine.

"Two tomorrow it is." Zac gave him a slight nod. "Sorry to have interrupted your evening."

With that, Zac disappeared into the crowd, leaving Giles with a bad feeling.

CHAPTER NINE

Heather's heart raced when she stepped into the Winter Festival Ball on Giles's arm. The grandeur of the event overwhelmed her. The marquee had been transformed into a magical winter wonderland, and she couldn't help but be captivated by the enchanting ambiance. She felt like a princess until Giles was pulled away by a man Heather had never seen before. As she got to the table where her family and close family friends were gathered, she was greeted by everyone who complimented her on her gown.

"My grandmother picked it out," Heather told everyone currently gaping at her like they'd never seen her dressed up before.

"I have great taste," Priscilla boasted, looking around the room. "Where is Giles?"

"He bumped into someone he knew," Heather told them.

Her eyes fell on the corner Giles and the man had retreated to, and Heather wondered who the man was. Her brow furrowed as she watched the exchange between the two men, and she couldn't help but admire Giles, who looked dashing in his tuxedo. A warm smile crossed his face, and her heart flipped in her chest when she saw him turn and look at her. Their eyes met across the sea of people for a few seconds before the man pulled his attention away from Heather once again.

A server offered her a glass of champagne. When she turned back toward the table, Heather's attention was caught by the giant Christmas tree with a golden star on top of it. The tree sparkled with a thousand lights, and its ornaments glittered like stars in the night sky. A feeling of magic and wonder washed over her as her eyes traveled the room. She felt like she was in a fairy tale, and finally, she felt the spirit of Christmas fill her.

"This is incredible," she whispered to Emily, who was sitting beside her.

"I know." Emily's eyes sparkled with awe as she glanced around the room. "Gran knows how to throw the most magical balls and weddings."

"Sitting at this long table facing everyone else at the function makes me feel like I'm at one right now," Heather told her.

"We are the hosts of this function," Emily pointed out. "As the hosts, Gran says, we must face all our guests."

"Doesn't that make the guests who aren't facing us seem rude?" Heather grinned cheekily.

"Trust you to think of that!" Emily rolled her eyes at her cousin. "That man checked in this evening." She pointed to the man talking to Giles. "Luckily, we had the room Avery was using while she stayed here last week available." She frowned. "He asked me what room Giles was in. But I told him I couldn't give out that information but could let Giles know he was here, but he said he'd wait to find him at the dance."

"Who is he?" Heather looked at Emily curiously.

"Zac Shields from Los Angeles," Emily answered, her frown

deepening. "I think he's FBI as I saw his badge when he reached into his coat to get his wallet at the front desk."

"FBI?" Heather's brow creased in concern. "I wonder what he wants with Giles because he seemed adamant that they speak immediately."

"Probably something to do with Giles's ex-fiancées father." Avery, who was walking past, overheard their conversation. She took Giles's seat to get involved in the conversation. "Kinsley Bamford. Daughter of James Bamford, the development and investment mogul."

"Is he under investigation?" Emily asked before Heather could.

"Bamford Development and Investments are renowned for selling off-plan property," Avery explained. "The Bamford's have made a fortune doing this. They have an incredibly clever legal team and real estate agency that ensures any building oversights have no blowback on them."

"How wholesome of them." Heather hated companies like that.

She'd heard of people being seduced into buying a magnificent condo in a booming neighborhood at a steal. But then, when they move in, they find it's all window dressing, but by then, it's too late.

"Three years ago, one of their buildings collapsed, and many lives were lost," Avery told them. "Unfortunately, one of those families was a congressman's daughter, husband, and four-year-old son."

"I heard about that," Heather said, looking at Avery. "There was a lot of fall-out over that, especially when that congressman was the one helping the development company with permits, and so on."

"Yes, he was kicked out of office, and Bamford nearly went bankrupt," Avery continued. "Giles bailed the Bamford's out and now owns more than half of it. He also has his people monitoring the business dealings. Giles will have *no* part in shady dealings."

"I'm sure I read that it wasn't the first time that development company had something like that happen to them," Heather said. "They were operating under another name at the time and partnered with quite a big real estate firm."

"Yes, that's right," Avery confirmed. "But that was twenty years or so ago."

"I can't believe they'd let the company continue operating in any capacity after one disaster," Emily stated.

"You'll be amazed what someone can do when they're as well connected as someone like James Bamford is," Avery told her.

Their conversation was interrupted when they saw Giles walking toward them. Heather's breath caught in her throat, and her heart did a few joyous skips as their eyes met. Giles greeted everyone at the table.

"I was keeping your seat warm for you," Avery grinned at him as she slid out of his chair and went back to her own beside Ryder.

"Sorry about that interruption," Giles apologized to Heather.

"Who was that?" Heather asked curiously.

"Zac Shields," Giles answered. "I know his brother Liam."

"Ah!" Heather nodded, sipping her champagne.

Giles was saved from more of Heather's questions when a server popped up beside him to order his drinks.

"Would you dance with me?" Giles smiled warmly at her.

"Haven't we had this conversation about dancing?" Heather's pulse raced as Giles reached out and took her hand.

"As I recall, when I finally enticed you to dance, we had a wonderful time on the dance floor." His eyes darkened as their eyes locked.

"Okay," Heather accepted the invitation. "But only because you let me fly your helicopter."

She allowed him to help her up, ignoring the sharp pain that stung her injured calf.

"Then, by my count, you owe me a lot of dances this evening." Giles placed his hand on the small of her back, maneuvering her toward the dance floor.

Couples swirled around, their movements fluid and graceful. The music, performed by a live orchestra, filled the air with enchanting melodies. They found a place amidst the swirling couples, and Giles pulled her closer. They started to move together, guided by the orchestra's romantic tune.

Giles was an excellent dancer, and he moved with such grace that it made Heather feel like she was gliding on air. Their bodies pressed against each other, and the world around them disappeared, leaving only the two in a secluded bubble.

She looked up into Giles's eyes, and a shared smile passed between them. The warmth of his hand against her waist sent shivers down her spine, and she nestled closer, her head resting on his shoulder. They moved in perfect harmony. Their steps synchronized as if they had danced together for a lifetime as they danced in silence. Their connection was more powerful than words could ever express.

They were so engrossed in each other that they lost track of time as they danced from one song to another as the Winter Festival Ball weaved its enchanted magic around them. Heather was so caught up in the moment she ignored the burning ache in her calf as Giles swirled her around the floor. She was glad that her grandmother had picked out a dress that's hem swept over her ankles and relieved the dress's daring slit was on the opposite side to her injury. Heather wasn't ready to answer questions about her leg and didn't want her traumatic recovery to ruin her picture-postcard vacation.

Eventually, the orchestra took a break, and the dancers left the floor. Giles took Heather's hand as they walked back to their table. As Heather took her seat, she bumped her injured calf against the side of the chair and had to grit her teeth to keep from yelping. In all the excitement of the past few days, she'd forgotten to take the medication the doctor had prescribed, although she had kept the injury clean and bandaged. As the pain from knocking the wound calmed to a throb, Heather felt something warm trickle down the side of her calf. She knew without looking at it that it was blood.

Oh no! Heather glanced down, and to her horror, a bright red stain was soaking into the side of her dress. *Shoot!*

Heather glanced around the tent to find the restrooms and saw the sign pointing out the marquee and toward the lodge. She was about to excuse herself and sneak out of the side exit near their table when Priscilla and Ryder stood up and clinked their glasses to get everyone's attention.

Oh, bother! Heather hissed to herself and knew she needed Emily's help.

"Em, I need your help," Heather whispered.

"What's wrong?" Emily whispered back.

Heather's injured leg was on her right side, which was the side Emily was sitting on.

"I've cut my leg and need to get to the restroom to clean it up." Heather moved slightly so Emily could peek at the blood seeping onto the skirt of Heather's dress.

"Heather, that's a lot of blood for a mere cut," Emily's whisper was laced with concern.

"I need to get out of here," Heather told her.

"*We* need to get out of here," Emily corrected. "I'm coming with you to help you."

"There's no need," Heather assured her. "It's just a cut. I tend to bleed a lot."

"I'm coming with you!" Emily's voice brooked no argument.

Heather relented, knowing her secret was about to come out, and she nodded.

"Avery." Emily turned to get Avery's attention. "Heather and I need to go to the ladies—desperately. Can you cover for us?"

"Sure," Avery said with a nod.

"Giles, Emily, and I are slipping to the powder room," Heather whispered to him. "Did my Gran mention you'll be lighting the tree?"

"No!" Giles looked at her, surprised.

"We'll be quick and try to get back here before that," Heather told him. "My Gran likes to make speeches before the tree lighting and handing out the gift bags."

"Okay," Giles nodded. "Do you want me to stall the Christmas tree lighting?"

"No, it's fine," Emily answered as they stood.

Emily moved Heather to the back of the tent and covered her so no one could see the blood on her dress from her calf. They moved quickly through the chilly air without their coats and were nearly frozen when they got inside the lodge.

"Wow!" Heather shuddered. "It's freezing out there."

"Definitely not the clothes to be wearing for an evening

stroll," Emily said, guiding Heather toward the office. "I have a first aid kit in the office."

"I can do it, Em," Heather assured her.

"I don't want to alarm you," Emily told her, pointing to the floor. "But you're dripping blood."

"What!" Heather looked down and noticed the small dots of blood that had followed them into the office. "Shoot!"

"Sit!" Emily commanded, pulling out a chair.

Feeling lightheaded, Heather did as she was told, and Emily pushed another chair in front of her.

"Elevate the leg," Emily instructed. "How on earth did you manage to cut your leg open?"

Heather blew out a breath and closed her eyes for a few seconds, chewing her bottom lip.

"Em, I need to tell you something," Heather admitted.

Emily retrieved the first aid kit and stood looking at Heather questioningly.

Heather took another breath and lifted her dress to reveal the large medical dressing that covered her calf. It was seeping blood, and Emily's eyes widened in shock.

"What the heck, Heather!" Emily's eyes moved from the injury to look at her cousin in disbelief.

Heather told Emily what had happened, leaving nothing out, and by the end of the story, Emily was sitting beside Heather and gently peeling back the blood-stained dressing. As the angry scars came into view, Emily sucked in her breath. Three of the baby jaguar's claws had dug into her flesh, leaving their imprint in a curve that ran from the back to the side of her calf.

"What were you doing in the jungle?" Emily asked as she

disinfected the scar Heather had opened with a nail a few days ago.

"I had an assignment there, and while we were in the jungle, I got a call about the baby jaguar caught in a snare." Heather winced as Emily dabbed the wound. "What the heck are you putting on it? Acid?"

"Oh, don't be a baby!" Emily chided. "You get slashed by a baby jaguar and manage to find your way through the jungle in severe pain but are crying over a little sting."

"I had adrenaline spurring me on in the jungle," Heather pointed out. "Right now, I'm freezing and not in danger, so I'm feeling every dab of that cotton swab."

"Sorry," Emily said, closing the disinfectant. "I don't have a dressing large enough to cover all the scars, but I have two that will cover the one you've opened."

"Thank you," Heather breathed a sigh of relief. "You don't have a spare dress, do you."

She glanced at the blood on the side of hers.

"As a matter of fact, I do." Emily grinned. "And you're in luck as it's in Ryder's apartment, so we don't have to go traipsing in the snow to get it in our slinky formal dresses."

"It's not pink, is it?" Heather's brow creased. "You know I don't wear pink as it clashes with my hair."

"You don't wear pink because you don't like pink," Emily corrected. "And no, it's not pink. It's emerald and similar to the design of your dress."

"Will it cover my leg?" Heather asked.

"Yes, it's the same length as your dress but without the slit in the skirt," Emily applied antiseptic cream to Heather's wound and covered it with the dressings. "That should hold it."

She started putting the items back in the medical aid kit. "You must see a doctor about the scar you've opened."

"I have," Heather admitted. "I saw one while I was in Denver with Gran. He gave me some antibiotics and cream. I've used the cream but forgot about the pills."

"Heather!" Emily sighed in exasperation. "Bring them to me, and I'll make sure you take them."

"I promise I'll take them from tomorrow," Heather stood, her calf throbbing but not as severely as it was. "Thank you, Em."

"You're welcome." Emily packed the first aid kit away and cleaned the office before leading the way to Ryder's apartment, which was on the side of the lodge.

They entered the guest bedroom, and Emily pulled a dress bag from one of the closest.

"Here you go," Emily handed the bag to Heather. "Give me your dress when you're done, and I'll soak it to get the blood out."

"You're my hero." Heather breathed a sigh of relief.

As she carefully unzipped the dress bag, a soft rush of breath escaped her lips, and her eyes widened in awe at the sight that unfolded before her. Heather carefully stepped out of her dress and into the one Emily had loaned her. Once she had it, she turned to look at herself in the mirror.

The dress was an emerald masterpiece of simplicity and elegance. Its Bardot sleeves gracefully adorned Heather's shoulders, framing an off-the-shoulder neckline that exuded timeless allure. Delicate ruching below the neckline and across the chest added a subtle touch of sophistication, accentuating the grace of her décolletage and waist.

The skirt cascaded in gentle waves, tracing the curves of her body as it flowed downward. With each step, the hem of the dress flirted with the ground, creating a soft, ethereal pool of fabric that whispered secrets of elegance. The emerald hue of the dress was a vivid declaration of nature's beauty, and it complemented her every movement. Heather loved the dress her grandmother had picked out for her, but the dress Emily had loaned her was the one Heather would've picked for herself.

She left the bedroom to find Emily in the family bathroom dabbing the blood stain from Heather's dress. Emily turned when Heather entered and smiled.

"I knew that dress was perfect for you," Emily told her.

"You chose this dress for me?" Heather looked at her cousin in surprise.

"Yes." Emily nodded. "I bought it when Avery and I went to Silverthorne because I didn't think you'd get to buy a dress for the dance. I didn't realize Gran was buying you one."

"This is going to sound silly." Heather laughed. "But I'm glad I was forced to change my dress."

"I'll get this dress to the laundry," Emily walked back to the lodge with Heather behind her.

Once Heather's dress was taken care of, they borrowed two of Ryder's coats and returned to the dance.

"Emily, please don't tell anyone about my injury," Heather asked when they neared the marquee. "I will tell everyone, and I had planned to, after the festivities."

"Sure," Emily said with a nod. "If anyone asks, I spilled cocoa on your dress, and that's why you had to change it."

"Thanks, Em." Heather hugged her before they stepped into the marquee as Giles was about to light the Christmas tree.

Heather and Emily slipped into their seats as the tree twinkled to life. The marquee was bathed in a soft, enchanting glow from the myriad of lights adorning the tree. Ryder and Hank, standing near Giles, began distributing the Christmas gift bags to the eager attendees. The bags, decorated with festive ribbons and sparkling with holiday cheer, held the promise of surprises and warmth. Laughter and joyful chatter filled the air as each guest received their gift, enhancing the festive atmosphere.

Once the gifts were distributed, the evening continued. Only Giles commented on Heather's change of wardrobe.

"Are you planning another wardrobe change before the evening ends?" Giles teased her.

"I hope not." Heather laughed. "This is the last evening gown I have."

"You look just as beautiful in this one as you did in the last one," Giles complimented.

As the evening continued, they mingled with the locals and visitors from Frisco and the surrounding areas who had gathered for the dance. Laughter and cheerful conversations filled the air, and the night seemed to whirl by in a blur of joy and connection.

Suddenly, it was midnight, and Christmas Day had arrived, sparking Christmas cheer in the marquee. Priscilla took to the stage, and the crowd eagerly gathered around as she led them in a medley of well-known Christmas carols. The voices of the community united, creating a heartwarming symphony that resonated with the season's spirit.

An hour later, the festivities began to wind down, and slowly, the marquee emptied. Among those left were Heather, Giles, Emily, and Hank.

"It's been a long day!" Emily looked exhausted. "I'm ready to fall into bed and sleep until midday."

"As if your grandmother's going to allow that on Christmas day." Hank laughed, wrapping his arm around her shoulders.

"Your grandmother invited me to join the family for Christmas lunch," Giles told them.

"I was going to if she hadn't." Heather smiled at him.

"Then I guess we'll see you at lunch." Emily grabbed her coat, which Hank helped her into. "We're going to go home."

With goodbyes and well-wishes, Emily and Hank left the marquee, leaving Heather and Giles alone beneath the twinkle of the Christmas lights.

Giles offered his arm, a gesture filled with warmth and affection. "Can I walk you to your cabin?"

"I'd like that." Heather nodded, accepting his extended arm.

They strolled through the chilly night, their steps in rhythm with their beating hearts. The soft, powdery snow beneath their feet seemed to glisten like diamonds under the moonlight, enhancing the enchantment of the evening.

Finally, they arrived at Heather's grandmother's cabin. The warm, inviting glow of the cabin's windows contrasted with the wintry surroundings. Giles turned to Heather. His eyes filled with admiration. The air was thick with the promise of something beautiful waiting to be shared.

And in that magical moment, beneath the watchful eyes of the stars and the radiant moon, Giles leaned in and pressed his lips to Heather's. It was a kiss filled with tenderness and the magic of a Christmas night, binding two souls in a promise of what could be.

CHAPTER TEN

Despite the late night at the dance, Giles woke up early on Christmas morning. The festive spirit in the lodge was contagious, and he couldn't help but be drawn into the joyful atmosphere. However, his early morning run beckoned, and he slipped into his running gear.

The air was crisp, and he could see his breath as he ventured into the forest surrounding Mistletoe Lodge. Snow crunched beneath his feet, and the world was painted in shades of white and silver. It was a Christmas morning straight out of a postcard, the beauty of the landscape taking his breath away.

As he ran deeper into the woods, the rhythmic thudding of his footsteps against the snow and the calm of nature had a soothing effect on him. The forest seemed to come alive with a silent energy as if the very trees were whispering the secrets of Christmas.

As Giles continued his run, he suddenly came upon a small clearing. There, on a bench, sat Heather, her running outfit damp with sweat. But it wasn't the sweat that caught Giles's attention; it was the expression of pain on her face.

Heather appeared lost in thought, her gaze fixed on the distant trees. As he approached, Giles noticed something alarming. There was a trace of blood on the bottom of her running pants, and his concern deepened. He slowed his pace and cleared his throat to alert her to his presence.

Heather jumped, clearly startled, and quickly shifted her gaze from the woods to him. Her expression wavered between surprise and a valiant attempt to mask her discomfort.

"Giles," she said with a small smile, "I didn't expect to see you out here."

His eyes remained locked on the bloodstain, and he couldn't help but ask, "Is everything alright, Heather? You look like you're in pain."

She sighed, her shoulders slumping. "I'm fine. Just a small accident."

He approached the bench, his eyes narrowing in concern as he tried to make sense of the situation. "What happened?" he asked.

Heather hesitated as if weighing how much to reveal. "I cut my leg on a branch while running," she finally admitted.

Giles studied her face, searching for any signs of deception. Her expression seemed genuine, and yet something was nagging at him. He couldn't help but notice no tear or visible cut on her jogging pants despite the bloodstain.

For a moment, he considered pressing her further about the injury, but he decided not to.

"I see," he replied with a nod, trying to reassure her. "Are you sure you're okay?"

She nodded and shifted her leg to inspect the wound, wincing slightly. "It's not too bad. I'll clean it up when I get back to the cabin."

As they sat in the wintry silence of the forest, he couldn't help but marvel at the tranquil beauty of the Christmas morning, the snow-laden trees shimmering like crystal, and the world wrapped in a peaceful stillness.

Heather broke the spell, and Giles watched her rise to her feet and stretch before turning toward him.

"Would you like to continue running together?" Heather asked.

Her offer to continue their run together was met with hesitation. "I'd love to, but are you sure you should run with your leg in that condition?" Giles's voice carried a note of genuine worry as he rose beside her.

Heather brushed off his concern with a dismissive wave of her hand. "I'm fine," she insisted, a defiant spark in her eyes.

Her casual assurance did little to ease his concern. Especially when she shifted her weight and subtly favored her right leg, Giles could see the discomfort she was trying to conceal in her eyes.

He decided not to press the issue further as she obviously didn't want to make an issue of her injury.

To ease her pain and not make it into a thing, Giles suggested, "How about we continue on a brisk walk instead? It'll be easier on your leg, and we can still enjoy the morning while getting in some exercise."

Heather considered his suggestion for a moment, and then a sly grin tugged at her lips. "A walk? Are you worried that I'll leave you in the dust if we run?"

Giles chuckled, appreciating her playful spirit even in the face of discomfort. "Maybe just a little," he admitted. "But today, it wouldn't be a fair race because of your leg."

Heather's grin widened, "Fine, but this challenge is to be taken up at a later date," she conceded.

"You're on," Giles accepted the challenge as they began their walk.

Giles made a deliberate effort to keep their pace easy and comfortable, ensuring that Heather's leg wouldn't be strained. He decided to change the subject as they strolled through the snowy woods.

"What can you tell me about this forest?" he began.

"What do you want to know?" Heather glanced at him.

"It's obviously old as the trees seem to have stood the test of time and weathered their share of beatings from nature." Giles stopped and ran his hand over one of the tall giants guarding the area. "What kind of animals inhabit it? Are there any rare or interesting species?"

Heather's face lit up with enthusiasm, and the discomfort in her leg was momentarily forgotten as she delved into an explanation. "Well, the forest around Mistletoe Lodge is home to various wildlife. You'll find deer, foxes, and even the occasional bobcat. It's not uncommon to spot red-tailed hawks soaring above; if you're lucky, you might see a pine marten. They're elusive creatures." She smiled. "Since nineteen-ninety-one, there have only been about thirty reported sightings of them in Colorado."

"What the heck is a pine marten?" Giles's brow furrowed.

Heather chuckled. "Not many people know about the furry creature."

They continued their walk as the sun ascended higher in the sky, painting the morning with its golden rays. The snow-covered branches glistened in the newfound light. The hush of the forest was periodically broken by the soft crunch of their footsteps in the snow.

"They're a member of the weasel family," Heather continued. "They share many of the same coloring and traits as weasels and stoats but are much larger. About the size of a cat."

"Great!" Giles's brows rose. "So, they're a cat-sized weasel?"

"They are much cuter than weasels," Heather informed him. "They have long bushy tails and large round ears."

"What about bears?" Giles asked, listening with rapt attention, appreciating her knowledge of the surroundings.

"I guess there could be an odd black bear around." Heather shrugged. "But generally, they enter a state of torpor during winter." She saw the look of confusion flash in his eyes. "Torpor is a long, deep form of hibernation."

The forest came to life with every word she spoke, and he couldn't help but feel a newfound appreciation for the wilderness surrounding them.

"Ah, so a very deep sleep." Giles grinned as their eyes met. "Like sleeping beauty."

"Sure." Heather laughed at his analogy. "Only I don't think any prince is going to attempt to kiss them awake."

"No, I guess not," Giles agreed, his mind picturing the consequences of that. "Are there any other predators we should be looking out for in these woods?"

"Pine martens are hunters," Heather told him. "While they're not big enough to cause any serious damage to humans, you should still be wary of them—if you're lucky enough to come across one." She bit her lip in contemplation. "Then there are coyotes, red foxes, bobcats, and some coywolves."

"What is a coywolf?" Giles's brow furrowed as he sought to understand this new creature.

"It's a hybrid of a coyote and a wolf," Heather explained. "Although they're not native to this area, there have been a few sightings over the years. They tend to expand their territory in search of new food sources."

"Interesting," Giles mused, intrigued by the idea of such a hybrid species in the region.

Heather continued narrating as they walked, "Then there are raptors."

Giles nodded in recognition. "You mean like hawks and eagles?"

"Exactly," Heather confirmed. As if on cue, the resonant call of an eagle split the tranquil forest, leaving a lasting echo in their ears. The sound was a visceral reminder of the wild world surrounding them.

They reached the edge of the woods and looked up as the magnificent creature swooped above them. Giles marveled at the eagle's majestic wingspan, painted against a pristine blue sky backdrop. As they watched, he felt like the beauty of nature was unfolding around them, revealing the intricate and captivating web of life in the woods.

Heather's smile broadened as she watched the bird of prey. "That's Jasper."

Giles raised an eyebrow, intrigued. "Jasper?"

"Yes," Heather replied, her voice filled with fondness. "He's a bald eagle who's made Mistletoe Lake his home for eighteen years. I was just ten when I found him with a broken wing." She turned her gaze to Giles. "Our local vet and I nursed him back to health. He wasn't even a year old at the time."

"Did you name him?" Giles inquired.

Heather nodded. "Yup, it was my 'Name of the Month.' I had wanted to name a new foal Jasper, but sadly, the foal didn't make it." A tinge of sadness colored her voice. "Jasper seemed like a fitting name for a creature as noble as a bald eagle."

With a warm smile, Giles acknowledged, "I'm sorry about the foal. Do you think Jasper remembers you?"

Heather's eyes sparkled with nostalgia. "It seems that way. He tends to appear more when I'm around as if he's welcoming an old friend back to his territory." She looked up as the magnificent bird made another graceful sweep through the clear, blue sky, its call resonating high above them.

They left the enchanting forest behind and entered a sun-kissed meadow, basking in the tender morning light. The meadow's gentle curve gracefully sloped downward, leading to the site where the Winter Festival had enchanted the previous night, now deserted and serenely quiet. Past that, the vast expanse of Mistletoe Lodge's land unfurled, a mesmerizing panorama of nature's beauty.

Mistletoe's pristine lake sparkled like a precious gem, while the towering Tenmile mountain range embraced it, casting a protective shadow over this picturesque realm. The scene was an awe-inspiring masterpiece of tranquil beauty.

In that moment, Giles wished he possessed the talent to paint, to immortalize this breathtaking view on canvas through his eyes. Heather's stories enriched their walk, connecting Giles to the wilderness in ways he hadn't expected.

As Jasper soared above them, the scene felt like a harmonious tableau of nature and human connection. The captivating moment had etched itself into Giles' memory. It was destined to be revisited long after their walk concluded, just like his deepening affections for the fiery-haired, remarkably fascinating woman who walked beside him. All too soon, they came to Priscilla's cabin.

"This is me," Heather reminded him.

They stood staring into each other's eyes for a few seconds before the front door opened, and Priscilla stepped out, surprised to see them.

"Goodness, the two of you are up early," Priscilla exclaimed.

"We went for a run, Gran," Heather turned to greet her grandmother.

"Good morning, Priscilla," Giles greeted her with a warm smile as he noted her jogging outfit. "It's a lovely morning for a run."

"Oh, no!" Priscilla looked at him in horror. "I don't run. I'm meeting my book club at a cafe in Frisco for a brisk walk and Christmas breakfast." She smiled. "It's an annual tradition." She looked at her slim gold wristwatch. "I must rush off. I'm going to be late."

"Enjoy," Heather told her grandmother as Priscilla excused herself and hurried off.

"Would you like to join me for coffee and breakfast?" Giles extended the invitation to Heather.

"Sure," Heather accepted with a warm smile. "I just need half an hour to get ready."

"I'll meet you back here in thirty minutes then," Giles replied.

As they stood there, their gazes locked, an unspoken connection drew them together like an irresistible force. They found themselves wrapped in each other's arms, their lips meeting in a soul-stirring, lingering kiss. The world around them seemed to fade away.

Jasper's call from above broke the spell, and they reluctantly drew apart. Giles smiled as they both looked up to see Jasper circling overhead, almost like a disapproving parent, overseeing their romantic moment.

"I think someone's jealous," Giles pointed out.

Heather laughed as she stepped away from Giles. "He's just being protective." She pointed to the cabin and started to move toward it. "I'll see you in thirty minutes."

Giles nodded and watched as Heather walked into the cabin. Concern creased his brow as he couldn't help but notice her slight limp. She waved at him before closing the front door. He turned and jogged back toward his cabin, accompanied by Jasper, who circled above as if ensuring he got home safely.

As Giles opened the cabin door, he was immediately drawn to a magnificent bird of prey perched gracefully on a nearby tree. The bird's piercing gaze felt like it was dissecting Giles's soul, sending shivers down his spine. He couldn't help but think that Jasper, the eagle, was intently watching him, assessing his presence.

"I promise you, I have no intention of harming Heather," Giles said to the regal bird as if the eagle could understand his words. In response, Jasper let out a haunting cry, almost as if acknowledging Giles's pledge. "So, you can stop giving me the eagle eye," he added, a wry smile playing on his lips, appreciating the irony of the idiom.

The sudden appearance of Avery broke his reverie.

"Avery!" Giles greeted her with genuine delight. "You look positively radiant."

Avery chuckled, giving an exaggerated curtsey. "Thank you. And you, my friend, look like you've been engaging in vigorous physical activity."

Giles nodded. "I went for a run."

Avery's eyes sparkled mischievously as she asked, "Did you happen to run into Heather while on your jog?"

Giles nodded with a knowing grin. "As a matter of fact, I did." He frowned. "Did you run into Priscilla on your way here?"

Avery's curiosity piqued, and she raised an eyebrow. "No. Why do you ask?"

"I wondered why you asked me about meeting Heather while on my run." Giles lifted an eyebrow.

Avery gestured towards Jasper, who still maintained his watchful perch in the tree.

"He's Heather's feathered protector, and he's been watching you." She looked at him teasingly. "And you were talking to him."

Giles couldn't help but feel intrigued. "So, Jasper remembers Heather?"

Avery nodded and divulged, "Heather raised him. Whenever she's around, Jasper tends to fly around the lodge and follow her like some sort of guardian."

Giles shifted his gaze back to the eagle. "Is he safe to be around?" he asked warily.

"I wouldn't try to touch him," Avery responded. "He is a wild eagle." She looked at Jasper. "I figure he could cause some serious damage if he wanted to. Have you seen those talons and that beak?"

Giles chuckled, "Not up close and personal, no." He shook his head.

Avery flashed a grin. "I wouldn't recommend it." Her features turned serious. "I'm sorry to barge in on you early on Christmas morning." She moved the subject away from Jasper.

"But I wanted to catch you before Ryder and I left for our honeymoon."

"You're not barging in at all," Giles reassured Avery. "I'm glad you came to visit, and Merry Christmas."

"Merry Christmas, Giles." Avery leaned in and kissed his cheek before saying graciously, "I wanted to thank you for everything you've done for Mistletoe Lodge and the Carlisles."

"I should thank you for introducing me to the Carlisles and Mistletoe Lodge." Giles offered her a drink, but Avery declined.

"I can't stay for long. I have to get back to the lodge as we're leaving in thirty minutes," Avery told him.

"Where are you headed for your honeymoon?" Giles asked, opening a bottle of water.

Avery clarified, "It's not our actual honeymoon. Ryder and I are going to Los Angeles for two weeks." She smiled at the look of surprise on his face.

"Ah, I see," Giles responded.

It hadn't hit home until that moment what it meant that Avery had married Ryder. Of course, she'd be leaving Los Angeles.

"I'm going to clean out my office at work and wrap up some things," Avery explained. "I've already quit, and luckily, I have a buyer for my apartment."

Giles recalled a potential buyer from their past discussions. "Is Jack Warren still interested in buying it?"

Avery's eyes sparkled with excitement. "Yes! I messaged him this morning, and he responded within minutes. It looks like my old apartment will finally have a new owner."

Giles couldn't help but feel a tinge of melancholy as he considered Avery's move. "Los Angeles won't be the same without you, Avery."

"I hope we'll see more of you here in Frisco," Avery told him, glancing at the clock over the kitchen door. "I'd better get going."

"Everyone seems in such a hurry on Christmas mornings here in Frisco," Giles joked.

"Says the man that never slows down." Avery laughed.

They hugged, and Avery left Giles standing, staring out the door, watching her walk through the snow back toward the lodge. Every step she took was symbolic of the distance Giles felt growing between their friendship now that she was married. Giles smiled. He was happy for Avery as he knew she'd never fully gotten over Ryder, and now their lives were joined, and she was happy.

Giles went to shower and get ready to meet Heather. He was about to walk out his cabin door when his phone rang. Giles looked at it and saw it was Kinsley. He didn't want to have to deal with her, so he hit the call decline button. He noticed a message from Barb and read it.

Merry Christmas from Oscar and me. I've booked a flight to Denver for tomorrow morning. I have arranged a car to collect us from the airport and drive us to Mistletoe Lodge.

Have a great day.

Giles smiled and replied.

Merry Christmas to you and Oscar. Have a safe trip tomorrow.

Enjoy your Christmas.

Giles

He was about to pocket his phone when it rang once again. It was Kinsley. Giles sighed and knew she'd keep calling if he didn't answer.

"Hello," Giles answered.

"Where have you been?" Kinsley sounded furious. "I've been calling you since midnight."

"Busy!" Giles told her. "Merry Christmas to you, too, Kinsley." His voice dripped with disdain. "I take it that is why you were calling? To wish me Merry Christmas as I don't know of another reason you'd be."

"I went past your house last night, and you weren't there," Kinsley fumed. "Your shrewish housekeeping wouldn't tell me where you were."

"Because it's none of your business," Giles pointed out. "What do you want, Kinsley?"

"I thought we could spend today together," Kinsley said sulkily.

"Why on earth would you think that?" Giles felt his anger stir. "We are no longer together."

"Come now, darling," Kinsley's voice changed to a purr. "When are we going to move past this?"

Giles's jaw clenched and he stopped walking. "Kinsley, if all you called for was to try and convince me to get back together with you, I'm afraid you've wasted your time."

"Everyone deserves a second chance!" Kinsley snarled. "You owe me a second chance."

"I don't owe you anything, Kinsley," Giles responded, his frustration palpable. He wondered what was wrong with her that she didn't understand. "I don't know how to be any clearer —we're over, and I have no desire to rekindle our relationship."

"You're going to live to regret this!" Kinsley sneered and hung up.

Giles exhaled as he stared at his phone for a few seconds before shaking his head.

"What is Kinsley up to?" Giles wondered aloud, but his

attention was caught when he saw Zac Shield walking toward him.

"Hi, Giles. Do you have a minute?" Zac asked.

"No, really," Giles said, his eyes narrowing as annoyance zapped through him.

"I just need to ask you a few questions," Zac assured him.

"Fine," Giles relented. "But please be quick, as I'm meeting someone in a few minutes."

Zac nodded and held up some photos he had in hand.

"Do you know any of these people?" Zac handed the photos to Giles.

Giles took the photos and looked through them. His eyes narrowed when they came to a picture of a woman he recognized.

"I've seen her somewhere before," Giles told Zac. "I'm not sure where."

"That's Janine Pook," Zac told him. "Does that name ring any bells?"

"Nope!" Giles shook his head. "I'll try to remember where I've seen her before." He looked at Zac questioningly. "Why do you have her picture?"

"Because she's involved with Gordon Jackson, the name behind the fraudulent foundation that used your company's name," Zac told him.

"Can I keep this?" Giles asked, holding up the photos. "When my assistant arrives here tomorrow, I'll ask her."

"Keep all the photos," Zac told him. "Maybe your assistant knows a few others in that pile."

With that, Zac left Giles staring after him. There was something in Zac's look when he referred to Giles's assistant that deepened the frown on Giles's face.

CHAPTER ELEVEN

Heather sat on her bed, staring at her aching, swollen calf. The wound on the torn open scar was not looking good—it was infected.

"Great, just great!" Heather muttered.

She picked up the cream the doctor had prescribed her and gently dabbed it over the wound before covering it with a dressing. Once dressed in jeans, a turtleneck shirt, warm socks, and boots, Heather took the pills she should've taken for the last two days.

Has it only been two days since I met Giles? Heather was amazed as it felt like she'd known him for much longer.

She couldn't believe how quickly she'd fallen for him, and even though Heather hadn't trusted him when she'd first found out who he was, after spending the past few days with him, Heather had come to trust him. She was convinced Giles was a man of honor and integrity who was always willing to lend a helping hand. He was also kind, gentle, and caring.

Unsurprisingly, she'd fallen for him and had known it when they had their first dance in the cozy all-night cafe in Denver.

While Heather wasn't an expert on reading relationship cues, she felt that Giles had feelings for her too—at least, she hoped he did. Heather frowned, thinking about what a relationship with Giles would be like or how it would even work as they were both busy, career-oriented people.

Her ex-fiancé and her both worked with conservation and wildlife. They understood each other's commitments but couldn't make their relationship work. A cold sweat popped onto Heather's brow as her mind whirled, screaming at her to put the brakes on with Giles while her heart fought against that advice because the instant connection Heather and Giles had didn't come around often in life.

A knock on the front door drew her from her thoughts, and her heart skipped a beat, knowing it was Giles. Heather collected her gloves, hat, and coat as she headed for the door. She swung the door open with a big smile, which instantly faded when she saw the man who'd approached Giles at the dance the previous night standing there.

"Hello, Miss Jessop," Zac greeted her. "Merry Christmas."

"Hi." Heather greeted the man, a frown creasing her brow. "Merry Christmas."

"I'm sorry to bother you on Christmas day," Zac said. "But I need your help." He introduced himself. "I'm Zac Shields with the FBI." He showed her his badge.

"You were speaking to Giles at the dance last night," Heather's eyes narrowed questioningly. "Why?"

"We're looking into a matter which concerns his corporation," Zac alarmed Heather by saying.

"I'm not sure how I can help you with that," Heather told him. "I don't know Giles that well, and I don't know anything about this company."

"But you do know about the Wildlife Guardians Foundation," Zac pointed out.

"Yes, I do." Heather nodded, and she realized that Zac must be investigating the foundation for Giles. Her frown deepened, and she wondered why the FBI would investigate that for him. "Why would the FBI be involved with an investigation into a foundation?"

"I can't disclose that information," Zac told her and moved to the conversation as to why he was there. "Could you tell me who you dealt with at the foundation?"

"Gordon Jackson and his partner Janine Pook," Heather answered.

"Did you ever meet either of them in person?" Zac asked her.

"Yes." Heather nodded. "I met both of them."

"Would you mind looking at a few photos and telling me if you recognize anyone?" Zac handed her the photos in his hand.

Heather took them and flipped through the pictures, picking out two.

"This is Gordon Jackson." Heather handed Zac the photo and then the next one, saying, "This is Janine Pook."

Zac's brow creased into a deep frown as he looked at the two photos and then back at Heather, "Are you sure?"

"Positive," Heather told him and looked up to see Giles walking toward them. "Is that all? I'm on my way to breakfast."

"Yes, thank you for your time, Miss Jessop." Zac gave her a slight nod. "Have a wonderful Christmas Day.

"Thank you," Heather said, barely registering when Zac left as her attention was on Giles.

She watched the two men greet each other as they passed.

"'What did Zac want?" Giles asked, turning to look at the man.

"He wanted me to identify some people I met from the Wildlife Guardians Foundation," Heather told him.

"Oh?" Giles's brow lifted as he looked at her with interest. "And did you identify them?"

"Yes," Heather said, with a nod, stepping out the door and pulling it closed behind her. "I picked Gordon Jackson and Janine Pook from the photos."

Heather was about to walk on but stopped as Giles caught her arm to stop her.

"Did you say Janine Pook?" Giles asked, his eyes widening in disbelief.

"Do you know her?" Heather's brows creased, and she felt her heart start to thud. *Is Giles involved with that awful foundation?*

"I'm afraid I do," Giles answered her honestly, closed his eyes, shook his head, and blew out a breath before looking toward Zac, who was becoming a spot on the horizon. "That's where I'd seen the woman in Zac's photo earlier."

"Oh!" Heather looked at him, surprised. "He showed you photos as well?"

"He did." Giles nodded. His eyes clouded with concern. "Was the woman you identified as Janine Pook wearing a gray suit and pink shirt, and she had dark bobbed hair?"

"Yes, that's the woman," Heather confirmed.

She started walking toward the lodge, and Giles followed next to her. Heather needed to sit as her leg ached, and she was starving.

"Does Janine Pook work for you?" Heather asked.

"No." Giles shook his head. "I don't know her. I know of

her." He looked at Heather questioningly. "What was her job for the foundation?"

"Janine was Gordon's partner," Heather told him, and his frown deepened.

Before she could say more, a cry from above them split the air, and they looked up to see Jasper flying above them.

"I see your feathered guardian is back." Giles laughed. "Jasper followed me to my cabin and sat outside glaring at me from a tree."

"I'm sure he was just ensuring you were safe," Heather stuck up for her friend.

They walked into the lodge, and the scent of breakfast wafted from the dining room, making Heather's stomach rumble. Luckily, it wasn't too loud, and the noise of festive lodge guests toned it out. They were ushered to a table by one of the lodge's regular servers, and as Heather slid into the chair opposite Giles, she felt a dull headache starting.

Great! Heather thought as she listened to the breakfast specials. *All I need is a migraine on top of my throbbing leg.*

"I'll just help myself to what's on the buffet table," Heather told the young woman.

"I'll do the same," Giles said.

"But I would like a cappuccino, please," Heather told the server.

"Anything for you, sir?" The server looked at Giles.

"I'll get a coffee from the buffet table," Giles said with a smile before the young woman nodded and left them.

After getting their breakfast, they sat eating in silence for a few minutes.

"What am I to expect for Christmas lunch today?" Giles broke the silence.

"If my Gran keeps to our traditions, we gather in her living room, and she breaks us into teams." Heather grinned at the look of surprise on Giles's face. "We usually have a *lot* more people over for Christmas lunch, but this year, it's just the six of us."

"Why do we get broken into teams?" Giles frowned curiously.

"For the Christmas day competitions," Heather informed him, sitting back in her seat with her cappuccino.

"Christmas day competitions?" Giles looked pained. "Aren't you supposed to sit around the tree, hand out gifts, and once they're opened, have lunch?"

"Ha!" Heather harrumphed, her grin widening, and mischief sparkled in her eyes. "Not in the Carlisle's household."

"Don't hold me in suspense." Giles leaned forward on the table, intrigued.

"First, there's the snowman-building competition," Heather told him. "My Gran has secret boxes filled with snowman decorations and clothing. You have to blindly choose a box and then make the most of the items you get to make your snow awesome."

"I love building snowmen," Giles told her.

"There's something you need to know about my family," Heather warned him. "We are *all* very competitive, even Rosie." She rolled her eyes and pulled a face. "Let me tell you, my Gran is the most competitive of all. She usually doesn't participate, but she'll team up with Rosie this year."

"Won't she know which box has the best stuff in?" Giles sat back.

"No, Nora, the Lodge's chef, will take over Gran's judging position," Heather explained.

"Why doesn't Nora rather team up with Rosie and let your gran maintain her position?" Giles teased her.

"Because Nora refuses to participate in any competition, friendly or otherwise, with my family," Heather told him. "She learned her lesson a long time ago."

"Ah!" Giles nodded. "Maybe I should offer to be the judge."

"Gran won't allow that." Heather laughed. "She'll insist you partake in the day's festivities."

"I'll be sure to gear myself up ready for some stark competition." Giles grinned.

"We used to have a toboggan race, but my Gran stopped it after there was an accident." Heather pulled a naughty face. "It seems someone cheated and sabotaged a few of the sleds."

"Would that have been you?" Giles guessed.

"No!" Heather looked at him innocently. "I have no idea why my sled was the only one that wasn't tampered with."

"So, you're telling me that you like to cheat." Giles laughed.

"No!" Heather emphasized the word. "But I was blamed, and now my grandmother only allows games during Christmas, New Year, and Easter that you can't cheat at."

Heather's head started to pound a little harder. Her eyes landed on her half-eaten breakfast, which she'd usually polish off, but the pain in her head had made her lose her appetite. Heather made a mental note to get some aspirin when she returned to Gran's cabin.

"What other festivities occur before we open gifts and eat?" Giles asked.

"There's the snowball fight," Heather told him. "We're each given a few snowballs, and the team that gets the most hits with the snowballs wins. Of course, you can ask for a few more, but one team member has to stop playing for every five added snowballs."

"I gather it's not going to be one team member for only five snowballs this year, as only six of us are playing?" Giles asked.

"I'm not sure how my gran plans on doing that." Heather shrugged. "The last game is the scavenger hunt." She rubbed the back of her neck. "It's usually held in the orchard. Each team gets clues and sections of the orchard they are allowed to search in. If a clue takes you into another team's territory, you have to pay them with sweets to enter."

"Ah!" Giles nodded. "So I take it we get sweets along with our clues and map?"

"Yes, but once again, you only have a limited number of sweets," Heather told him and smiled. "You can try and sneak onto the other team's territory, but if you're caught, you have to pay a penalty in sweets. The winner of the hunt has to find all their items and have the most sweets left."

"That sounds like fun," Giles said. "I do like a good scavenger hunt, and I have no idea when last I went on one." He frowned as if trying to remember. "I take it the rules for the hunt are your grandmothers?"

"Yup!" Heather nodded. "My Gran missed her calling in life. She should've been an event planner."

"I think you're right about that," Giles agreed. "She put together a beautiful small wedding for Avery and Ryder in a couple of hours, and the dance was magical."

"My Gran used to throw me and my cousins the most awesome birthday parties when we were young," Heather told him. "Kids used to fight to get invited to our parties."

"When my mother still had her bakery and we lived in our

old neighborhood, we too had amazing street parties for our birthdays," Giles told her.

"Have you been back to your old neighborhood since your family moved away from it?" Heather leaned back as the server took their breakfast plates and cups away.

"I have," Giles answered with a nod. "It's so different now."

"I'd like to see it sometime," Heather told him.

"When we're back in Los Angeles, I can take you there," Giles offered.

"That would be great," Heather said, and though she didn't want their time together to end so soon, her head was starting to pound like someone was playing a bass drum in it.

Heather was trying to think of an excuse to leave and was saved by the ringing of Giles's phone. He looked at the caller ID, which she read from her side of the table as Barb.

"Sorry, Heather, I have to take this. It's business," Giles apologized. "I'll meet you at your Gran's cabin for lunch?"

Heather didn't even blink about him conducting business on Christmas day. When she wasn't home with her family, Heather was usually working on the day.

"Of course," Heather said, secretly relieved.

Giles stood, "Hello, can I call you back in ten minutes?" After he hung up, he leaned over and kissed her cheek. "Sorry for being rude. I'll see you later."

"Not a problem," Heather assured him and watched him rush out of the dining room.

She looked at her wristwatch. She still had a couple of hours to get rid of her headache before her Gran came home and the Christmas festivities began. A few minutes later, she let herself into her grandmother's cabin and had just made it through the door when she needed to throw up and just made it to the bathroom.

After losing all of her breakfast, Heather found some aspirin in her grandmother's bathroom cabinet. She took a few pills with a cold bottle of water and lay down for an hour. Her eyes had just drifted shut when there was a knock on the door.

"Aghhhh!" Heather groaned, pulling a pillow over her head, planning to ignore the intruder.

But whoever it was persisted, and Heather had to answer it. She yanked the door open, and her eyes widened in surprise. The most gorgeous red, white, and gold sleigh she'd ever seen was parked outside her grandmother's cabin.

"What on earth!" Heather breathed, spellbound by the load of presents stacked inside it. "Is Santa somewhere here, too?" She grinned at Hank. "He's a little late, isn't he?"

"Hey, Heather. Merry Christmas," Hank greeted her, laughing at her silliness. But his smile turned into a frown when he noticed how pale she was. "Are you okay?"

"Hi Hank, Merry Christmas," Heather returned the greeting with her eyes plastered on the sleigh. "Where did you get your new transport from?"

"Beautiful, isn't it?" Hank said, stepping aside so Heather could examine it. "It's a gift to the lodge, and yes, it came loaded with gifts from Giles."

"Giles?" Heather stopped and gaped at Hank before returning her attention to the sleigh. "Who are all those presents for?"

"Us, the lodge's staff, and the guests," Hank told her. "Each present is labeled with our guests' names on them too."

"When did he have time to do this?" Heather marveled, running her hand over the beautiful craftsmanship of the sleigh.

She stopped walking around it to look at Hank, frowning. "How did you get it here?"

She looked around, expecting to see reindeer or at least horses.

"With Dinah." Hank pointed to the big yellow tractor.

"That's cheating, and so not in the spirit of Christmas," Heather pointed out teasingly.

"What were you expecting me to pull it with?" Hank asked her. "I can't pull that thing. The sleigh alone is too heavy and even more so ladened with gifts."

"What?" Heather looked at him in feigned disappointment. "No reindeer?"

"First, you'd be the first one to moan at me about using reindeer to pull this thing, and you'd probably free them," Hank pointed out. "And secondly, when did you last see a reindeer around these parts?"

"Good point," Heather said before grinning. "But now that we have this sleigh, maybe a few will fly in to pull it."

Hank sighed and rolled his eyes in disgust.

"Why have you brought it to Gran's cabin?" Heather moved the conversation along.

"Because she ordered me to," Hank told her. "She wants me to hook up some of the horses to the sleigh, get dressed in the suit that came with it, and ride it to the lodge after lunch to dish out the presents."

Heather looked at Hank, wide-eyed, pursing her lips, trying hard not to laugh as she pictured Hank in a Santa suit driving the sleigh.

"Don't you dare laugh, Heather!" Hank warned her, his eyes narrowing. "Or I'll think of some way to get you to be Santa and drive this thing."

"Can I?" Heather asked, genuinely intrigued and willing to do it.

"Most definitely not!" Priscilla's voice cracked like a whip from behind them, making them spin around to see her staring at them.

"Ah, Gran!" Heather said pretending to moan like a child having a tantrum. "But I want to be Santa and drive the sleigh."

"I want Heather to be Santa and drive the sleigh, too," Hank joined her.

"I'll put both of you on a time-out if you carry on this silliness," Priscilla tried to keep her tone stern, but laughter twinkled in her eyes. "But Heather can be Santa's helping elf." She pulled two elf costumes from the sleigh. "Emily can be one, too, and all three of you can ride in the sleigh."

"What?" Emily spluttered. Her arms were ladled with parcels as she made her way to Pricilla's cottage. She was eyeing the Elf suit in disgust. "There's no way I'm being an elf." She glanced at the sleigh. "Nor am I riding in that!"

"Ah, come on, Em!" Heather and Hank pleaded in unison. "It's going to be loads of fun."

"I promise it's not like the hay ride cart," Hank promised her and glared at Heather. "And Heather can't push you off. Especially if you're sitting in the middle."

"Spoilsport." Heather pulled a tongue at Hank, enjoying the playful Christmas banter.

"Ooh, can I be an elf and ride on the sleigh too?" Rosie appeared from behind Emily.

"Of course, sweetheart," Priscilla said. "We still have your elf costume from the pageant you did last month."

"Yay! I can wear the costume again!" Rosie clapped her hands gleefully, jumping up and down.

"Well, that's settled then, and it will be a fun activity for after lunch," Priscilla told them and looked around. "Where's Giles?"

"He had to take care of some business," Heather answered, rubbing her temples.

"Are you alright, sweetheart?" Priscilla's brow furrowed in concern.

"Yes, Gran, I'm fine," Heather assured her. "I've got a bit of a head cold from running around in the freezing cold in a strappy dress last night."

"Have you taken some aspirin?" Emily asked, her eyes narrowing, and Heather noticed Emily glance toward Heather's injured calf.

"I did," Heather said, nodding, and looked accusingly at Hank. "I was lying down for an hour when Hank turned up with the sleigh ladened with gifts."

"Why don't you go lie down until we're ready to start the festivities, sweetheart," Priscilla suggested. "You want to enjoy the day, and there's nothing worse than trying to do so with an awful headache."

"I'll be okay, Gran," Heather told her. "I can feel the aspirin starting to work," she lied.

"Come on." Emily dumped the parcels she was carrying in Hank's hands, linked her arm through Heather's, and then walked her into the cabin. "Let's get your head sorted out."

"I'm telling you, I'm fine." Heather tried to reassure Emily, but she ignored Heather and marched her into Heather's bedroom, closing the door.

Before she could protest, Emily touched her forehead, and her eyes widened.

"Heather, you're quite warm," Emily said worriedly.

"It's probably because I've been sleeping in this oven of a cabin," Heather started to feel stuffy and pulled off her sweater. "Phew. That's better."

"Let me see your leg," Emily demanded.

"It's all better," Heather lied once again. "I cleaned it and redressed it before I went for breakfast and took the pills the doctor gave me."

"We're not leaving this room until I've looked at your leg!" Emily said stubbornly, moving in front of the door and folding her arms across her chest.

"Fine!" Heather relented and took off her jeans to show Emily her leg.

Emily gently pulled back the dressing and sucked in a breath. "It's infected, Heather."

"I know!" Heather told her. "But it's fine. Now that I've taken the tablets and used the cream, it's not as painful as it was a couple of hours ago."

"We need to get you to a doctor, Heather," Emily insisted.

"I'll go the day after tomorrow when everything opens again," Heather promised.

"I don't like this," Emily told her, gently applying more cream and folding the dressing back over the wound. While Heather dressed, Emily said, "We're going to the doctor tomorrow. You can see Dr. Reed in Frisco."

"He's a GP," Heather pointed out.

"And qualified to either treat the wound or send you to someone who can." Emily raised her eyebrows. "Even if it means hospitalization."

"Oh no!" Heather shook her head emphatically. "I am *not* going back to the hospital. I've had my quota of them for the next twenty years."

"That's too bad!" Emily turned to open the door. "Because if the doctor says that's what you need, I'll hog tie you if I have to, to drag you there.

"How lovely." Heather threw her hands in the air. "Fine, we can go to Doctor Reed tomorrow."

"I'll make the appointment." Emily pulled the door open and walked out of the room.

Heather followed closely, her heart racing as the sound of Giles's laughter reached her ears. As Heather stepped into the living room, their eyes locked in a moment that spoke volumes without words.

CHAPTER TWELVE

The afternoon had flown by in a blur of fun, laughter, giving, good food, and excellent company. Giles couldn't remember when he'd had such a good time with real down-to-earth people. The sleigh he'd managed to organize when he'd gone to Denver for Avery's wedding was a hit and was now proudly displayed by the giant Christmas tree that twinkled over the lodge.

They sat with the last lingering guests in the lodge's living room. Hank was Santa, while Heather, Emily, and Rosie were his elf helpers. They had dished out gifts to the lodge's guests. They were enjoying decadent hot chocolate drinks around the fire, and Christmas day was nearing an end.

"Are you sure you're alright?" Giles frowned worriedly at Heather. "You've hardly touched your toffee caramel hot chocolate."

"I'm tired," Heather admitted, stifling a yawn and glancing at her wristwatch. "I'm sorry to be a party pooper, but I'm going to turn in early."

"How's your headache?" Priscilla had overheard their conversation and turned to look at Heather.

"It's fine, Gran," Heather told her with a small smile.

Giles's frown deepened as his mind went over the day. He remembered thinking more than once that Heather didn't seem to be her usually energetic self. She'd been trying to hide it and put on a show, but Giles had noticed she wasn't as bubbly as usual. His eyes fell to where Heather said a branch had nicked her leg that morning. Giles was sure it was much worse than a nick, as she'd favored that leg the entire day.

Giles watched Heather intently, noticing her eyes had a sheen over them like she was running a high temperature. Worry zipped through him, but he pushed it aside.

"As I said earlier, I've probably caught a bit of a chill from running in the cold evening air without my cloak last night," Heather explained, then looked at Giles. "I'm going to call it a night."

"I'll walk you to your cabin," Giles said, standing with her.

"You don't have to," Heather told him. "Stay. Finish your hot chocolate and relax by the fire."

"I'd rather walk with you," Giles told her, his voice becoming low and gruff.

They said their goodnights, grabbed their coats, hats, scarves, and gloves on the way out of the lodge, and once they were wrapped warmly, stepped into the brisk night. Giles saw Heather shiver. He took his coat off and wrapped it around her before pulling her close to his side.

"You're freezing," Giles noted.

"I must be coming down with flu," Heather told him, cuddling into him.

"I noticed you weren't as energetic as usual," Giles

commented. "You should've said you weren't feeling well and not pushed yourself like you did."

"Nah!" Heather shook her head and grinned. "I was having a good time. I can be sick tomorrow."

"You really are amazing." Giles kissed the top of her head and was alarmed to feel how hot her face was even in the cold. "Heather, I think you have a fever."

"No," Heather denied. "It's just my cap that makes my head hot."

"You need to get into bed and sleep," Giles suggested as they arrived at Priscilla's cabin.

Heather opened the door and turned to him.

"Thank you for walking me home and for a great day," Heather said.

"I had the best time I've had in a long time," Giles told her.

He pulled her to him and kissed her. Feeling how warm Heather was, Giles didn't prolong the kiss.

"Goodnight, Giles," Heather's voice was soft as she turned and walked inside the cabin, turning to wave.

"Goodnight, Heather," Giles waved back and watched as the door closed before turning to walk to his cabin.

Giles didn't realize until a cold shiver ran through him that Heather still had his coat. He was about to turn back but decided he didn't need it. His cabin wasn't that far. As he walked towards his cabin he worried about Heather as he knew she had a slight fever, but Giles had come to know Heather well enough to know you couldn't push her into admitting anything she didn't want to. Giles's lips spread into a smile, thinking about how stubborn she could be. His musings were interrupted when he saw the lights on in his cabin and shadows of movement from within. Giles crept up to the cabin and cautiously opened the door. He entered the cabin silently, creeping up on the intruder in the kitchen.

He looked around for a weapon to use. The only thing Giles could see was the fire poker. He snuck over and picked it up before creeping back to the kitchen. Giles's back flattened against the door. He took a breath and sprung into action with poker raised in readiness, startling the blond woman who was about to take a sip of water.

Giles froze, staring at the woman in disbelief as she screamed in fright. The bottle of water sloshed its contents all over her designer outfit before hitting the floor. Giles lowered the poker, his emotions running from relief to annoyance and then red-hot anger.

"Kinsley!" Giles hissed. "What are you doing here?"

"Being scared to death by *you!*" Kinsley breathed, holding her chest as the fear started to subside, and then her eyes landed on the weapon in his hand. "Were you going to hit me with that?"

Giles looked at the poker and put it on the counter before getting a tea towel to clean up the mess Kinsley had made with the water.

"I thought you were a burglar," Giles growled, cleaning up the spilled water and retrieving the bottle. "What are you doing here, Kinsley?"

He wrung the tea towel out over the sink and laid it out to dry before turning to glare at her.

"Daddy and I are meeting my mother in Breckenridge," Kinsley told him. "Daddy needs to talk to you, and I volunteered to come tell you."

"How long have you been here?" Giles walked out of the kitchen with Kinsley following him.

"About half an hour," Kinsley told her. "The concierge let me into your cabin. I told her I was your fiancée, come to surprise you for Christmas."

"Why would you do that?" Giles asked through gritted teeth.

"Because I was hoping maybe it would be true again?" Kinsley smiled seductively at him. "We were good together, Giles, and I miss you."

"It's over, Kinsley," Giles stated. "You need to get it through your head that we're over and are *never* getting back together." He put more wood on the fire before turning toward her again. "Besides, I've met someone else."

"Here?" Kinsley looked at him in disbelief and said nastily, "A country bumpkin?" Her eyes narrowed. "Who is she?"

"That's none of your business," Giles told her before changing the subject. "What does your father want that can't wait until I'm back in Los Angeles after New Year?"

"All Daddy would tell me was that it's urgent." Kinsley shrugged and looked at her wet clothes. "I'm freezing. Thanks to you scaring me half to death, I'm all wet."

"I'm sure once you have your coat on and you're back in whatever town car brought you here, you'll get warm again," Giles said, unconcerned, looking at his wristwatch. "It's getting late. You should get on your way back to Breckenridge."

"Oh. The car won't be back until the morning to collect both of us," Kinsley said, smiling sweetly. "So I'm stuck here for the night."

"I'll order you a cab," Giles snarled. He was about to get his phone and remembered it was in his coat pocket.

"Don't bother, there won't be any cabs in this part of the world this late on Christmas day," Kinsley pointed out smugly.

"You can stay in the guest bedroom," Giles was not amused by her antics.

"Do you have something for me to sleep in?" Kinsley asked him, pointing toward her clothes. "I can't sleep in this. It's all wet."

"I'll get you one of my shirts," Giles told her, walking to his bedroom and pulling out one of his cotton shirts. He returned to the living room, where she stood waiting for him. "Here. There's a dryer in the kitchen you can put your clothes in."

"Thank you," Kinsley said. "Which bedroom can I use?"

"Take the first one on the left," Giles instructed, picking up the landline phone and dialing the lodge's front desk.

"What are you doing?" Kinsley asked as she walked toward the room.

"Calling the front desk to get a car for you first thing in the morning," Giles answered.

"You have to come with me," Kinsley stopped at the bedroom door.

"Your father has my phone number to call and schedule an appointment," Giles informed her. "Tell him to do that, as I already have a full day tomorrow."

"He's not going to be pleased!" Kinsley's eyes flashed with annoyance.

"That's not my problem, and I *don't* answer to *your* father." The front desk answered the call, and Giles organized a car for Kinsley.

He was about to get ready for bed when Kinsley popped out of her room wearing his shirt with her clothes in her hand.

"Would you help me with the dryer?" Kinsley asked him.

At first, Giles thought she was joking. "You've never used a dryer?"

"I haven't needed to," Kinsley told him.

"Give me your clothes!" Giles snatched them for her hands and went to shove them in the dryer. "When they are done. Simply open the door and take them out."

"I know that!" Kinsley glared at him. "You need to come with me tomorrow as Daddy is expecting you."

"Like I said, your father can call me and schedule an appointment." Giles walked past Kinsley, and that's when he noticed his laptop was open. He stopped and frowned. Turning toward her. "Did you use my laptop?"

"No!" Kinsley denied, looking at him in disbelief.

Giles didn't want to get into an argument about it. He closed it and took it with him.

"I'm going to bed," Giles informed her. "Your car will be here at seven to take you to Breckenridge."

"Whatever!" Kinsley waved her hand in the air and walked toward the bedroom Giles had assigned her.

He turned to go when a thought occurred to him, and turned to Kinsley.

"Did you say you were meeting your mother in Breckenridge?" Giles frowned. "I thought you and your father hadn't spoken to her in years?" His frown deepened. "Didn't she walk out on you and your father when you were ten?"

"Yes," Kinsley confirmed with a nod. "But Daddy keeps in contact with her as they're still in business together." She pulled a non-concerned face. "I don't see her often, but when I found out you were in Frisco, I came to Colorado with Daddy to meet up with her." She looked at him as an idea struck her. "You could meet her tomorrow if you came with me."

"I'm not interested in meeting your mother, Kinsley," Giles told her flatly. "Goodnight."

He turned and walked into his room, closing and locking his bedroom door, wondering how Kinsley and her father had found out where he was. Only Barb and Todd knew where he was; he was sure neither would've told her. Although it wasn't a secret, Giles just didn't like being stalked.

———

Heather woke early the next day. Her head was still pounding, and her leg felt like it was on fire. Heather didn't have to look at it to know it was inflamed. She found her phone and called Emily.

"Heather?" Emily's voice was gravelly from sleep. "Are you okay?"

"Sorry to wake you so early," Heather's voice was soft as she didn't want her grandmother to hear her. "But I need your help."

"Is it your leg?" Emily guessed right away.

"Yes," Heather admitted. "I need to get to a doctor today."

"I'll call Doctor Reed. I have his emergency number," Emily offered. "You know you'll have to tell everyone about this now?"

"Let's see what the doctor says first," Heather suggested.

"Fine," Emily agreed. "I'll call you back in a few minutes."

They hung up, and Heather cautiously pulled the dressing off her leg and drew in a breath when she saw how infected it was.

"Great!" Heather mumbled, pocketing her phone and quietly going to the bathroom.

While she waited for Emily, Heather took a quick shower and redressed the wound. She was dressed and waiting by the time Emily called her back.

"That was more than a few minutes," Heather pointed out.

"Sorry, I had to wait for the doctor to call me back," Emily told her. "Can you get to the lodge in thirty minutes?"

"Yes, I'll come over now," Heather told her as her eyes landed on Giles's coat. "I want to pop past Giles's and give him back his coat he lent me last night." She grinned as she heard a ring coming from one of the pockets. "And I think I have his phone too."

"You should just let him and Gran know that we're going to the doctor because you have the flu," Emily suggested.

"I don't want to cause a panic for nothing," Heather said. "I promise if it's serious, I'll let them know when we return to the lodge after the appointment."

"I'll hold you to that," Emily told her. "I must get ready."

"Okay." Heather ended the call.

She wrote a note for Priscilla.

Gone to Frisco with Emily - Heather x

Heather quietly let herself out of the cabin and forced herself to walk as normally as possible toward Giles's cabin. She came down too hard on her sore leg and nearly stumbled. Giles's coat fell, and his phone dropped out of his pocket. Heather fumbled in the snow to pick it up and retrieved his jacket. She was drying his phone off when Stacy, one of the lodge's front desk administration staff.

"Good morning, Heather," Stacy greeted her cheerfully. "Where are you off to so early?"

"I'm going to Giles," Heather told her absently as she wiped the snow from Giles's phone.

"Oh, can you give him a message please?" Stacy asked. "I was on my way there, but if you're going..."

"Sure," Heather said. "But why didn't you just call his cabin?"

"I think the phone must be off the hook," Stacy told her. "The call isn't going through, and his mobile is just ringing and ringing."

"Maybe he knocked the phone cabin phone off the hook." Heather grinned as she glanced at the phone in her hand. *It must've been Stacy calling a few minutes ago.* "I'll give him the message."

"Great. Can you tell Giles his fiancée's car will be here in forty minutes," Stacy's words stunned her, and she looked at the woman in confusion.

"His fiancée?" Heather's brows furrowed as a whooshing sound filled her ears, and tiny little pinpricks of shock stung her nerve edges.

"Yes, she arrived here last night," Stacy continued, not realizing that her words felt like bullets piercing Heather's heart.

"I'll let him know," Heather managed to say and was unsure why she offered to instead of running in the opposite direction.

"Thank you," Stacy breathed a sigh of relief. "My shift has ended, and I'm exhausted. I just want to get home."

"Go home," Heather forced a smile and tried to act as natural as possible, hoping Stacy couldn't see the turmoil raging inside her. "And drive safely."

"Thanks, Heather," Stacy said before returning to the lodge.

Heather's heart pounded against her rib cage while the world felt like it had closed in around her, and disbelief coursed through her. Giles had mentioned he'd been engaged but had told her he'd ended the engagement over a year ago.

Did he lie to me? Heather glanced at his phone.

Her fingers clicked the phone on as if on their own accord,

and her eyes widened at the messages stacked up on the screen. The ones that stood out the most were the ones from Kinsley Bamford.

Darling, where are you? I'm in your cabin waiting for you with your Christmas gift.

Pain clasped her heart with its sharp talons and ripped through it straight to her soul before baring down on her chest, making it hard to breathe, and the world started to spin. Heather fought back the tears burning at the back of her eyes and rasping against her throat. Her knees began to feel weak as if they were about to buckle.

A cry split the air from above before a shadow descended over her, and Jasper landed in front of her, letting out a softer chirp as he settled a few feet in front of her. The distraction had jolted Heather from falling into an agonizing heap with her heart bleeding out in the snow. Jasper gave another soft cry as Heather's breathing righted itself, and she felt she could walk again and swiped away the few tears that had managed to escape.

"Hey, Jasper." Heather sucked in a shaky breath, steadying herself. "You always seem to appear when I need you."

Jasper gave another soft cry, flapping his amazing wings. He turned his head from side to side as if ensuring Heather was alright before lifting himself into the air with another cry.

"Thank you," Heather called after him, watching him soar into the heavens above her and circle around.

Heather wanted to dump Giles's things in the snow and march off to meet Emily, but she forced herself to go to his cabin and see for herself that he was a lying, cheating snake. She let herself remember the project in Africa for which his company had pulled the funding and let herself feed off that anger, ignoring Giles's claim that he knew nothing about it. If he'd lied about his engagement, he sure could have lied about that.

Heather squared her shoulders, lifted her chin, and walked towards Giles's cabin, icing over her feelings for him. He was a lying cheat, and Heather didn't have time for people like that. As Heather made her way to Giles's cabin, her feathered guardian flew above her, keeping a vigilant eye on her, letting her know she wasn't alone—that comforted her.

When Heather got to Giles' cabin, her leg felt like it had been in a bushfire while inside, her emotions were toiling about like they were rolling down a hill laden with thorns. She didn't allow herself to hesitate as she knocked on his door and had to contain the spark of anger and pain that ripped through her when a rumpled blonde woman in one of Giles's shirts answered the door.

"Can I help you?" The blonde woman looked at Heather down her snooty nose.

"Is Giles here?" Heather asked, keeping herself calm and her emotions steady.

"He's in the shower." The blonde purred. "Can I give him a message?"

"I need to check his cabin phone," Heather told her through gritted teeth.

"Oh?" The blonde's eyebrows rose. "Why?"

"The front desk has been trying to call him." Heather didn't wait for the woman to invite her in.

She pushed past her and walked into the cabin.

"That's rude!" The blonde hissed and stalked after Heather.

Heather was shaking with anger but forced it down as she

walked to the phone. It was off the hook. Heather picked it up and slammed it back onto the cradle.

"You are *not* allowed to take the phones off the hook. It's for safety reasons," Heather told the woman.

She was about to dump Giles's coat on the dining table and storm out when he came down the hallway. Heather stopped, her eyes narrowed as more anger spurted through his system. His hair glistened from the shower, and he was buttoning his shirt.

"Did I hear a knock on the door, Kins..." Giles's voice faded as he looked up from buttoning his shirt to see Heather glaring at him. "Heather!"

"Your car you ordered will be here in forty minutes." Heather shoved his coat at him. "This is yours." Giles looked at her, speechless, and took his coat. "This is also yours." She slapped the phone into his hand. "As I told your *guest*, you can't take the cabin phone off the hook."

"Heather—" Giles tried to say something, but Heather spun on her heel. "Wait."

She turned. "Sorry, I'm late for an appointment because *you* took your phone off the hook!"

With that, Heather fled his cabin, ignoring the pain searing through her leg and bleeding her heart. By the time she got to the lodge, tears stained her cheeks.

"Heather, wait!" Giles called behind her, but Heather continued walking. "Heather—" Jasper's cry made her glance around. "What the..." he muttered. "Darn bird!"

Heather saw Jasper make a few threatening swoops at Giles as if warning him to stay away from Heather. Only when Giles stopped walking did Jasper fly off and perch on a branch to watch Giles warningly.

Heather turned and continued toward the lodge, stopping a few feet away from the front door to gather herself, wiping away the tears, and taking a few deep breaths. Ignoring her painful leg, pounding head, and bleeding heart, she squared her shoulders and limped into the lodge.

Emily was on her way out of the office when she spotted Heather. Her eyes widened, and concern darkened them as she hurried forward.

"Heather," Emily said, touching Heather's arm. "What's wrong? Are you feeling worse?"

"Can we go?" Heather asked, hanging on to what little control she had left.

"Sure," Emily nodded and walked them out of the lodge to her car. "I had Hank bring the car around and warm it up for us."

They were pulling out of the drive as a town car pulled in, and Heather gave in to the pain burning through her leg, head, and heart as she did something she rarely did and burst into tears.

CHAPTER THIRTEEN

iles stood in the snow, confusion coursing through him as he watched Heather hurry away. He wanted to follow her, but Heather's pesky feathered protector wouldn't let him. Every time Giles went to walk toward the lodge, Jasper flapped his menacing wings warningly.

Giles's jaw clenched as he turned to return to the cabin and get rid of Kinsley. He realized he was still holding his coat and phone. He glanced at the phone and froze at the message he saw on the screen from Kinsley, and his blood started to boil. It was time to get rid of Kinsley once and for all.

Giles stormed into the cabin to find Kinsley perched on a chair, sipping coffee around the dining table.

"That front desk woman was very rude!" Kinsley stated.

"That *wasn't* the front desk administrator," Giles corrected her curtly. "That was one of the *owners*."

"Oh!" Kinsley pursed her lips. "Still, she was very rude. Barging in here and ordering me to put the phone back on the hook."

"Why was the phone off the hook?" Giles looked at her accusingly.

"It must've fallen off." Kinsley glanced away from him and took another sip of coffee.

"You need to get dressed," Giles ordered. "Your car will be here soon."

"Will you change your mind about coming with me?" Kinsley pouted. "Please."

"No!" Giles put an end to the conversation. "If you're not dressed in ten minutes, I'll call security to remove you from my cabin."

"What is with you?" Kinsley's attitude changed and she scraped the chair back standing. "You're being very unreasonable and downright rude."

"Everyone is rude, according to you, Kinsley." Giles ran a hand through his hair, checking his phone. He found a message from Barb. She was already on her way to the lodge. "Ten minutes."

Giles tapped his watch and stalked through to his bedroom.

"My father's not going to be happy that you're not coming back with me," Kinsley shouted down the hallway.

"I don't care," Giles said, closing his bedroom door to call Barb.

They needed to talk about the developments on the fraudulent foundation. He hit dial on Barb's number, and she answered after the fourth ring.

"Hey!" Barb greeted him. "This drive is breathtaking."

"Yes, it's a lovely part of the country," Giles agreed.

"Uh-oh!" Barb said, realizing by his tone that something was wrong. "What's up?"

"Where do I start!" Giles gritted his teeth. "How long until you're here?"

"We should be there in an hour," Barb told him.

"Great," Giles said. "You'll stay in my cabin for a few nights until a few guests leave."

"Where are you going to stay?" Barb asked him.

"I'll be staying in Ryder and Avery's house, which is attached to the lodge," Giles told her.

"Okay," Barb said. "I'll see you in about an hour."

"Good," Giles said, nodding. "We need to talk as soon as possible when you get here. It's about the fraudulent foundation."

"Sure," Barb said. "I'm sure Oscar can amuse himself for a while."

"I'll organize something for him," Giles promised.

"Thank you," Barb said, and they ended the call.

Giles let out a breath. He felt like his life had become a series of landmines that he kept stepping on. Giles needed to talk to Heather. He tried her number, but it went to voicemail. He closed his eyes and shook his head. A knock on his door distracted him.

Giles stood and went to answer it.

"There's a man here to see you," Kinsley told him before flouncing down the hallway.

Giles frowned and walked after her, stopping when he saw Zac waiting for him in the living room.

"Hi," Zac greeted. "I need to have a word."

"Sure," Giles said, any distraction was welcome.

"My car should be here soon," Kinsley gathered her things. "I'll go wait at the lodge." She looked at Giles. "You'll be hearing from my father."

With that, she turned and stalked out of the cabin.

"Was that Kinsley Bamford?" Zac asked although Giles didn't know why he asked when the man clearly knew who she was.

"Yes," Giles confirmed with a nod. "I believe Heather identified Gordon Jackson and his partner Janine Pook?"

"She did." Zac nodded. "That's why I'm here. To let you know that based on Heather's identifying them and the documents she presented to us, we have enough evidence to build a case."

"Are you sure Gordon's partner is Janine Pook?" Giles asked. He didn't want to believe she'd be involved with the fraudulent foundation.

"I do have something for you to look at," Zac didn't answer Giles's question and handed him some documents. "Can you tell me if this is your signature?"

Giles took the document, frowning when he saw it was the business documents for the Wildlife Guardians Foundation. His eyes fell to the bottom of the page and widened. There on the page was his signature. He flipped the page and saw his signature on the subsequent pages. As Giles flipped through the pages, his heart grew heavier and heavier as the truth glared at him.

"It's my signature," Giles confirmed. "But if I had to guess, I'd say my signature stamp was used on each page. The signature is perfect."

"We figured that." Zac nodded. "Which brings me to my next question."

"Who has access to my stamp?" Giles swallowed and ran a hand over his face. *No, it couldn't be true. But the evidence was staking up.*

Giles told Zac who would have access to it.

"Are you sure?" Zac's brows were drawn together as he stared at Giles. "No one else could've had access to your signature stamp?"

"No." Giles shook his head. "It's locked in the safe in my office."

"I see." Zac nodded. "I have a few more leads to follow up on, and I'll let you know when we're ready to close in on the fraudsters."

"Can I be there when you do?" Giles asked.

"I don't think so," Zac told him. "I must go."

"Thanks for the information." Giles looked at the documents. "Do you have a copy of this document and the photo of Janine Pook for me?"

"Sure," Zac said. "You can keep this document." He pulled some photos from an envelope and handed Giles the one of Janine Pook.

Zac left and Giles flopped onto the sofa slapping the foundation documentation and the photo on the coffee table. He glanced at his wristwatch. Giles still had some time before Barb and Oscar arrived. He could find Heather and explain what Kinsley was doing there.

Giles went to Priscilla's cabin only to discover that Heather and Emily had gone to Frisco. Frustrated, Giles made his way to the lodge and found Kinsley waiting in the living room. She was talking to Zac. Giles was about to walk over to find out what they were talking about when a car pulled up outside, and the concierge went to call Kinsley.

"Did you come to see me off?" Kinsley smiled prettily at Giles as she walked into the foyer.

"No," Giles said, shaking his head. "I came to get something to eat."

"I could stay and have breakfast with you," Kinsley offered.

"No thanks," Giles declined her offer. "But I will walk you out to ensure you leave."

"How nice!" Kinsley said sarcastically as she led the way through the front doors and to the waiting car.

The driver was holding the back door open for her. As they neared the car, another car pulled into the driveway. Kinsley turned to look at the vehicle before flinging herself into Giles's arms and kissing him. Giles was so stunned it took him a few seconds to push her way.

"Stop it!" Giles hissed, his eyes flashing with anger.

"Just a kiss goodbye." Kinsley gave him a smug smile before slipping into the backseat.

The driver closed the door and went to get into the driver's seat, then pulled off.

"She's really something," Zac appeared next to Giles. "And vindictive."

Giles looked at Zac and followed his gaze. Giles froze, and his heart dropped when he saw Emily standing glaring at him. He looked behind her, feeling disappointed when he didn't see Heather.

"Good luck!" Zac patted Giles's shoulder before walking off.

"So it's true!" Emily glared at Giles. "You know my cousin trusted you and she hasn't trusted anyone since that sleaze of an ex-fiance of hers broke her heart four years ago."

"Emily, it's not what it looked like," Giles told her.

"No, it never is." Emily shook her head in disgust. "Now, if you'll excuse me, I must pack for Heather."

"Pack?" Giles's heart dropped further in his chest. "Where

is she going?"

"She's being transported to Denver General," Emily told him.

Her words sent shock waves of concern through him.

"I knew she had a fever last night!" Giles said. "Where is she now?"

"Didn't you hear what I said?" Emily shook her head. "Medic-Vac is transporting Heather. She's already gone."

"What's wrong?" Giles asked.

"I'm sorry, but I won't have you upsetting my cousin any more than you already have with your lies and deceit." Emily's eyes narrowed, and spat sparks at him. "Right now, she doesn't need more pain than she's already in."

"Pain?" Giles ignored Emily's animosity. All he could think of at that moment was that Heather was being airlifted to hospital, which could only mean whatever was wrong with her was severe enough to warrant that. "Is it her leg? I know she caught it on a branch while jogging."

Emily harrumphed. "You have no idea what the state of her leg is." She moved past him, but Giles stopped her by catching her arm.

"Please, Emily, I need to know," Giles's voice was hoarse with emotion.

Emily looked pointedly at the iron grip he had on her arm, and he quickly let go. "Heather's injury isn't from a twig. It's from the claws of a baby jaguar she rescued while on a mission in the Amazon."

"What?" Giles's face scrunched in confusion.

Emily gave him a brief overview of what had happened. "Heather ripped the one scar open on a rusty nail while helping us put the booths for the fair together."

"And she left it until it became infected." Giles closed his eyes and shook his head. He opened them and looked at Emily. "I need to go see her."

"She doesn't want to see you," Emily told him. "So, no."

"Will you at least tell her I'm thinking about her?" Giles pleaded. "I promise you. What you witnessed was nothing."

"It looked like something to me." Emily's brow creased. "And Heather filled me in on what she found when she was at your cabin this morning."

"It's not like that!" Giles exclaimed and was distracted when a car pulled up.

Barb and Oscar bundled out.

"Is this my welcome party?" Barb beamed as the driver got their luggage from the trunk.

Barb and Oscar walked toward Giles.

"Wow!" Emily's eyes widened knowingly. "I'm glad Heather saw you for what you were so early in your relationship."

With that, Emily turned and walked off, leaving Giles staring after her in frustration. This day just got worse and worse, and he felt like he'd got tangled in a web of misunderstandings.

"What was that about?" Barb looked at Giles questioningly.

"Hello, Mr. Giles," Oscar greeted Giles and shook his hand.

"Hey, Oscar. How was your flight?" Giles turned his attention to the young man.

"Awesome," Oscar told him.

Giles got Barb signed in and managed to organize someone from the lodge to look after Oscar while he and Barb met. He'd decided to hold the meeting in Ryder's house, where Giles would be staying for a few nights while Barb was at the lodge.

Once Barb and Oscar were settled in and the sitter arrived, Barb arrived at Ryder's house.

"Would you like something to drink or eat?" Giles asked.

He knew he was stalling as he was not looking forward to this meeting.

"No, I'm good, thanks," Barb declined the offer.

"Take a seat." Giles sat on one of the sofas in Ryder's living room, and Barb sat in an armchair across from him.

Barb's eyes narrowed suspiciously. "What is going on with you?"

"There's no easy way to do this." Giles ran a hand through his hair, pulled out the foundation documents, and handed them to her. "Do you recognize these?"

Barb's frown deepened as she took the documents from him and scanned through them before looking at him.

"They're for the Wildlife Guardians Foundation." Barb scanned them again. "And they have your signature stamp on them."

"How do you know that?" Giles looked at her expectantly.

"Because each signature is perfect, and your signature never looks this perfect," Barb told him and handed the documents back to him. "Do you think someone got hold of your signature stamp to open the fraudulent foundation?"

"Barb, please," Giles's voice dropped as he looked at her. "I know."

"Know what?" Barb looked at him in confusion.

"I know it was you that did this." Giles held up the documents.

Barb's face fell and paled as her eyes widened in shock as she stared at him, her mouth dropping slightly open.

"Excuse me?" Barb spluttered after a few seconds of gaping

at Giles.

"Heather identified the people she had contact with from the foundation," Giles informed Barb and turned over the photo he had upside down on the coffee. "This was one of the partners—Janine Pook."

The name made Barb's eyebrows rise and head jolt as if she'd been slapped.

"This is the woman Heather identified." Giles pointed at the picture. "I was asked by the FBI agent looking into the case to identify some of the culprits and saw the photo of the woman. But at first, I couldn't place where I'd seen her before." He swallowed as he felt physically ill that someone like Barb, whom he'd trusted more than anyone, had betrayed him. "When Heather told me the woman's name, I knew where I'd seen her. The picture on your desk—she's your mother."

"My mother!" Barb spluttered once again, her eyes widening further. She glanced at the photo. "You think that's my mother?"

Barb snatched up the photo and looked at it.

"Your mother's name is Janine Pook, isn't it?" Giles pointed out. He was trying to keep calm. Everyone deserved a chance to defend their actions.

"Yes." Barb nodded. "My mother's name is Janine Pook."

"She was working with a man named Gordon Jackson." Giles looked at Barb curiously when she squeaked upon hearing the man's name.

"Gordon Jackson?" Barb asked in disbelief. "Is this some sort of sick joke?" Her voice was laced with anger, which sparked in her eyes.

"No, I'm afraid not, Barb." Giles looked at her with a deep frown. "This is a very serious matter. The FBI is about to arrest them and anyone involved with this fraudulent foundation." His eyes scanned hers. "Gordon Jackson has been on the FBI's watch list for some time for this sort of thing."

"The FBI is closing in on my mother and Gordon Jackson?" Barb's anger flashed in her eyes. "Please tell me I'm being punked right now!"

"What's got into you?" Giles hissed in frustration. He'd been patient up until now, but Barb wasn't being cooperative while he was giving her a chance to tell him her side of the story. "Barb, the FBI is here, waiting for you."

"For me!" Barb pointed at herself. "Let me get this straight. Just for the record." Her eyes narrowed. "You're accusing *me* of using your signature stamp to authorize a fraudulent foundation set up by my mother and Gordon Jackson?"

"Barb, I'm trying to get your side of the story," Giles told her.

"It sounds like you've already got the story you want," Barb pointed out.

"No, I don't have the story I want." Giles shook his head, his eyes reflecting his sadness. "I want to hear you say that you had no choice and had to do this."

"I can't tell you that." Barb shook her head. "I shouldn't have to tell you that." She took a deep breath. "I'd have hoped you'd have known me well enough to know I didn't."

"Barb, please," Giles flopped against the back of the sofa. "I just want the truth."

Barb looked at him and nodded slowly.

"Here's a truth for you," Barb told him. "I quit." She stood. "You can return to your cabin as Oscar and I won't be staying."

"Barb, please, talk to me." Giles stood up and looked at her pleadingly. "I just want to know why you'd do this."

"Are you kidding me!" Barb finally snapped, her anger sparking up again. "You honestly think I'd do something like after all these years we've worked together?"

"The evidence is overwhelming." Giles scooped up the photo and looked at it before looking at her and asking. "Who is Gordon Jackson? And please don't try to deny you know him because as soon as I know, you recognize his name."

"Gordon Jackson is my father," Barb's words shocked him as he stared at her.

"What?" Giles gasped.

"Or rather, *was* my father," Barb told her.

"I thought your father was dead?" Giles asked her questioningly.

"He *is* dead!" Barb said. "So whoever the FBI is closing in on, it isn't my father." She snarled. "And here's another kicker for you." She snatched the photo from his hand. "This is *not* my mother. She may look like her, but it's not her." She yanked her locker from around her neck and opened it. "This is my mother." Her eyes misted over. "Or was my mother."

"I don't understand?" Giles said, staring at the locker and the woman in the photo. "Is this your mother's sister then?"

"My mother does have a twin sister, yes," Barb confirmed. "But I don't know her and never have. My mother was spurned by her family when she married my father. My grandfather tried everything he could to split them up." She shook her head. "Do you want to know why?"

Giles stood staring at Barb, dumbfounded, and nodded.

"My mother's family were the criminals, *not* my father," Barb explained, her voice filled with icy disdain. "When I was young, my father and mother gave the feds information that brought down my grandfather's criminal organization. We lived in witsec for years after that until eight years ago when my mother's family found us."

"Barb, I—" Giles began, only to be silenced by Barb holding up her hand.

"Do you know how I met Oscar's father?" Giles shook his head. "He was the agent assigned to get us out of Chicago, where we'd been staying when we were found. Before he could relocate all of us, my parents were both killed. Gunned down right in front of me." Her voice rose and her eyes darkened with emotion. "I was whisked away. Had to change my name once again."

"Your parents are dead?" Giles gave his head a shake as the implication of Barb's story hit him. "But the stamp and the names?"

"Do you think this is the first time my parent's names have been used?" Barb hissed. "My mother's sister and her brothers are still out there. Oscar's father was tracing them and trying to get them all behind bars so we could finally live without fear and be free."

"That's how he was killed?" Giles felt like a complete idiot. "I'm sorry, Barb."

"Not as sorry as I am." Barb shook her head, snatching her locket from Giles's hand. "I'll clear out my desk when you're back in Los Angeles."

"Barb, please don't leave," Giles pleaded with her. "I'm so sorry I ..."

"You thought I was the one behind a fraudulent foundation!" Barb finished for him. "I'm sorry, but I can't work for someone that thinks so little of me." She shook her head sadly. "We'll stay the night because Oscar is tired, but we'll leave as soon as we can tomorrow."

"Barb, please!" Giles tried to reason with her. "Let's speak about this."

"There's nothing to speak about," Barb said and turned to leave, stopping when she came face to face with a stunned Emily.

"Hi!" Emily greeted her sheepishly.

"Emily!" Giles breathed. "How long have you been there?"

"Uh—" Emily bit her lip. "A lot longer than I'm comfortable with. Someone needed to see Giles and was coming to get him. I've been here since you accused your..."

"Executive assistant," Barb told her, then glanced at Giles. "Sorry, ex-executive assistant."

Emily nodded and continued. "Ex-executive assistant of creating a fraudulent foundation." She frowned and turned to Barb. "Is that the one Heather worked on that caused all those deaths?"

"Yes," Barb answered before Giles could.

"I'm Emily, by the way," Emily introduced herself. "Part owner of the lodge."

"Hi, Barb Gardner," Barb introduced herself.

"Please don't leave," Emily implored Barb. "My niece has just met your son, and she's delighted to have another young person here." She smiled. "A room just opened up in the lodge, and you're welcome to stay there compliments of Mistletoe Lodge Management."

"That's very kind of you," Barb said. "I may just take you up on that offer. I need a vacation."

"Perfect," Emily told her. "I'll have Hank collect your things and move them to the room."

"Thank you." Barb smiled gratefully before turning to Giles. "I'm not the *only* one who had full access to your office or knows the combination to the safe in your office." She turned back to Emily. "I'm glad we met."

"Me too," Emily said before Barb could leave. Zac stepped into the room.

"YOU!" Barb hissed. "You're the FBI agent on this case?"

"Hi, Barb," Zac's voice dropped as he greeted her. "How are you?"

"A lot worse now that I know you're here." Barb pushed past Zac and stalked out of the room.

"Zac needed to see you," Emily told him. "Now, if you'll excuse me, I must find Hank."

Emily disappeared down the hallway, and Giles dropped his head back and stared up at the ceiling before flopping onto the sofa in defeat.

"This day just gets worse and worse." Giles rubbed his hands over his face before looking at Zac who took the chair Barb had vacated. "I guess you overheard my conversation with Barb?"

"I did." Zac nodded.

"You know, Barb?" Giles looked at him questioningly.

"Yes," Zac confirmed. "And yes. But I didn't think you'd actually accuse her of being the one behind the fraudulent foundation."

"How do you know Barb?" Giles was curious.

Zac sighed, and it was his turn to flop back against the chair. "Her late fiancé was my partner. I was with him when he was killed protecting me because I got shot by being reckless." His jaw clenched. "Not only was Trevor, Barb's late fiancé, killed, but her mother's family that we'd finally closed in on got away."

"That's why she looked at you like she hated you." Giles nodded in understanding.

"Well, it looks like we're now both members of that club,"

Zac pointed out. "I've been keeping an eye on Barb and Oscar since Trevor's death. I promised Trevor I'd look out for Barb and his unborn child when he lay dying in my arms."

"That's why you're so interested in this case," Giles realized and shook his head. "If that's not Barb's mother, who is it, and who is the other Gordon Jackson?"

"I can answer that for you," Zac told him. "And thanks to you, we have Barb's mother's family gathered in one place and are about to take them into custody." He grinned. "I thought I'd come let you know, and I was hoping Barb was with you so she'd know too."

"Wait!" Something in Zac's voice and eyes struck a chord with Giles. "You're in love with her."

"A lot of good that will do," Zac grunted, then held up the envelope. "These are the real fraudsters."

Giles took the envelope. His eyes widened in disbelief when he pulled the photos out.

"This is James Bamford, Brand Frampton, and Kinsley?" Giles looked at Zac in disbelief.

"Yup!" Zac nodded.

Suddenly, it made sense. Kinsely would've easily had access to his safe.

"Turns out they pushed Kinsley at you hoping to hook their wagon to a money-making benefactor," Zac explained. "The entire family has gathered in Breckenridge because Kinsley was sure she could lure you back."

"Great!" Giles didn't like feeling like a fool. "Who is this woman though?" He held the photo of the woman he thought was Janine Pook.

"Janine's twin sister, Gale. She's also Kinsley's mother." Zac's words nearly made Giles choke.

EPILOGUE

It was the last day of the year, and Heather had spent the best part of the last week in hospital. The one scar had never healed properly, and when she'd scraped it with the nail, it had made the already underlying problem worse. But it had healed, and the doctors were letting her go home in time for the new year.

Heather was impatient to get out of the hospital as she waited for her grandmother and Emily, who'd been staying in Denver to be near her, to collect her. She had to remain in the hospital room waiting for them. She flopped onto the bed as the last week played through her mind.

Giles had sent her message after message. Emily's new friend, Barb, who was Giles' executive assistant, had come to visit Heather on a few occasions while she was in hospital. Barb had given her the news about the fraudulent foundation and told her that Giles was setting up a project he'd like Heather and Barb to oversee and ensure the dam was built to standard and was a success.

Barb was happy to go to Africa, even if a particular FBI agent would accompany them. Even though most of Barb's mother's family had been captured, she still had an uncle in the wind, and the FBI was worried about Barb and Oscar, so Africa was a good place for them to lay low for a year. Emily had told Heather that she thought Zac was in love with Barb, although Heather was sure Barb didn't feel the same way about Zac.

Emily and Barb had both pleaded Giles's case for him. Emily's last parting words to Heather were, *'If Barb can forgive him for accusing her of fraud, surely you can find it in your heart to forgive Giles.'*

When Heather thought about it, there was nothing to forgive, and she knew she'd been the one who'd jumped to conclusions and thought the worst. Her bad experiences with relationships had clouded her judgment, and she hadn't given Giles a chance to explain. Guilt flooded her as she knew it had been easier to run and believe the worst than face him because it meant she had to admit to just how deeply she felt for him.

That terrified Heather. While she told people, she hardly remembered her parents, the truth was that she'd felt their loss deeply and still did. One minute, they were on their way home to her, and the next, they were never coming home again. Her family thought that when she and her ex-fiancé broke up, it had made her weary of relationships. But the fact was that Heather had come too close to letting another person in—someone who could be ripped from her in the blink of an eye. She'd been the one to sabotage that relationship.

When Heather had seen Kinsley in Giles's cabin, while it had hurt like salt in an open wound, a tiny part of her was relieved. It was better to lose him before she'd entirely given her heart to him. But Heather knew it was far too late for that as she'd given her heart to him the moment their eyes had met in the elevator that first day.

Her phone pinged and she picked up. Her heart skipped a beat when she saw a message from Giles.

Meet me under the mistletoe at the entrance of the marquee at midnight, and I'll know you've forgiven me. If not, I'll understand, and I'll be leaving Mistletoe right after midnight.

Heather—I'm sorry. But I never invited Kinsley to Frisco. We were over a long time ago, and I never felt for her what I feel for you.

Giles

Heather's face split into a smile, and her heart raced with anticipation as she glanced at the clock. It was almost seven in the evening. She craned her neck to see out the door.

"Where the heck is my family?" Heather grumbled. "I need to get home."

It was nearly nine-thirty when they finally arrived to get her. Heather was beside herself when Barb and Emily walked into the room.

"What the heck took you so long?" Heather growled. "I have to be at the lodge before midnight."

"Don't worry," Barb told her. "We have the helicopter."

Barb and Emily glanced at each other.

"Why do I feel there's a but?" Heather picked up her backpack.

"You have to sit in this." Emily pointed to the wheelchair she pushed into the room.

"No!" Heather shook her head.

"It's hospital policy," Emily stated.

"If I sit in it, will it get us out of here faster?" Heather grumbled and plopped herself in the wheelchair.

"We can get out of the hospital," Emily mused.

They exited the room.

"What was the but you were about to tell me?" Heather asked.

"We're not sure if we can fly as it's snowing," Barb told her.

"Great!" Heather hissed. "I need to get home before midnight."

"Why?" Emily asked. "Are you going to lose a glass slipper?"

"Yeah, let's go with that." Heather was not in the mood for her cousin to be cute. "I need to get to the lodge so I can apologize to Giles and tell him—"

"Tell him what?" Barb and Emily asked in unison.

"That I love him!" Heather admitted.

Emily stopped pushing as they got near the hospital doors. Heather looked back to see Emily and Barb look at each other and then at her.

"Well, then, let's get to the airport and hope we can fly home," Emily said.

As they drove through the Denver streets to the airport, Heather's heart felt heavy as she watched the snow fall around them. It didn't look good.

"Call him and tell him," Barb encouraged her.

"I tried to call him," Heather admitted. "But communication must be down as I can't get through."

"It's New Year," Emily pointed out. "The mobile towers get overloaded, and it's hard to get through to anyone." She glanced out the window. "This weather doesn't make it any easier."

When they arrived at the hangar where one of Giles's helicopters was, they were told they didn't have a pilot, or at least not one confident enough to fly through the snow.

"Is the helicopter ready?" Heather asked, watching the time tick away.

"Yes, but there's no pilot," one of the flight technicians told her.

"We have a pilot who *can* fly in these conditions," Heather told the man.

"Oh no, Heather!" Emily said, realizing what Heather was about to do. "You've just come out of hospital."

"And I'm as good as new." Heather ignored Emily's reservations.

Within twenty minutes, they'd taken off, and it was already after ten, which meant they were cutting it fine to get to the lodge by midnight.

As the countdown clock relentlessly ticked down to midnight, the helicopter descended upon the lodge. Heather's skilled piloting ensured a smooth landing in the familiar spot where her journey had begun. The night air was electric with anticipation, and the snowflakes danced around them, creating a sparkling backdrop to count in the new year.

Without a moment's hesitation, Heather leaped out of the helicopter and sprinted through the fresh snowfall. She ignored the aches in her leg and the concerned voices calling her name. Her heart beat in rhythm with the final moments of the year, urging her to reach her destination.

Amid the bright, bustling marquee, her frantic search ended as the countdown reached "four."

Her eyes found Giles and time seemed to stand still. In that electric moment, their souls connected, transcending the chaos of the room. Heather fought her way through the crowd as Giles moved toward her, determination etched on their faces.

Finally, their worlds collided as Giles swept her off her feet, and Heather's heart soared.

"Giles!" she whispered, her arms finding their place around his neck.

Their gazes locked. "I love you, Heather," Giles declared his love.

The words slipped past his lips to the loud chorus of "Happy New Year" cheers from the crowd. The world ceased to matter as Heather responded, her voice joining the chorus of celebration.

"I love you too," Heather declared, her eyes shimmering with emotion as Giles held her in his arms—where she knew without any doubt left in her heart was where she belonged.

Amidst the cacophony of jubilation, their lips met, sealing their love with a heart-stopping kiss that eclipsed everything around them. They were lost in each other as the new year began, marking a new chapter in their lives. Without words, they knew that whatever lay ahead from that moment forward, they would face it together.

THE END

I hope you enjoyed the story of Heather and Giles. Before you go it would mean so much to me if you could review this book on Amazon. An honest review is a great way to support my books and helps me to know what you enjoy to read the most. All you need to do is go to https://www.amazon.com/review/create-review/B0CKS6QFL5

. . .

Thank you so much!

Hugs,

Amy

WANT ANOTHER CHRISTMAS STORY?

To read Nantucket Christmas Escape go to
www.amazon.com/dp/B0C1F4SVBS

Three women at crossroads. One renewed friendship pact and a winter escape that will change their lives forever....

When Maggie inherits her grandfather's Nantucket cottage,

she realizes there's no one in her life to fill the walls of Hope Lodge with laughter and love.

Hoping she'd be married by this age to someone keeping her company when she retires from her career in publishing, Maggie decides to restore the place and put it on the market.

As the festive season of love draws near, Maggie starts to accept a life of loneliness ... Until she meets Stephen, the contractor renovating the lodge – a man she can hardly stand, but one with a heart of gold that warms hers like no other.

Suddenly, spending one last holiday in Hope Lodge with her two best friends she misses dearly, Holly and Cassie, doesn't seem like a bad idea...

When Holly lost her husband last Christmas, all meaning was drained from her life.

Can she find the will to start anew and trust her heart?

As a busy lawyer in Boston, Cassie hardly has time for her husband and son. Worst of all, she's certain Seth, her childhood sweetheart, is cheating on her.

They were looking for a festive season break of healing on the sleepy shores of Nantucket. But what happens when the three women discover so much more than they bargained for?

Get ready for a swirling, romantic winter adventure with Amazon's best-selling author, Amy Rafferty's heartwarming Christmas trilogy.

If you love second-chance romance, strong heroines, deep friendship and idyllic winter settings, the Nantucket Christmas Escape Trilogy is your ultimate Christmas read all year round!

Prepare for a magical journey where love and hope bloom without warning to warm the hearts of those who need it the most.

READ NANTUCKET CHRISTMAS ESCAPE TEASER BELOW...

CHAPTER 1

DECEMBER – ONE YEAR AGO – BOSTON, MA

Holly Wells stood staring at the Christmas tree framed in her living room window. The bright red, silver, blue, and gold baubles sparkled when the multi-colored fairy lights twinkled through them. The sound of voices was muffled behind her as she tried to let the happier memories of the past three weeks filter out the bad ones.

There are no bad memories of time spent with loved ones, Holly, only good ones and hard ones. The good ones are the band-aids that cover the wounds left by the hard ones. Don't mourn my death when the time comes, my love. Celebrate our time and journey together and treasure the time you have left. I know it will be hard for you when I'm gone, and you'll need time to heal. I don't want you to be alone while you are mending, so I got you a little friend named Harry.

Tears trickled unchecked down Holly's cheeks as her eyes dropped to the soft eleven-week-old bundle of fur asleep in her arms, her German Shepard puppy. At fifty-two, Holly had never imagined herself already a widow. She wiped her cheeks with the back of her hand as she heard footsteps approach her. Holly sniffed and quickly pulled herself together as she turned around.

"I've packed the dishwasher with the last of the dishes," Cassie Kendrick, one of Holly's lifelong best friends, walked up to her. Holly could see the compassionate concern in her friend's eyes and had to swallow down the lump burning the back of her throat. "The last of the guests from the funeral reception have left. Well, except for Maggie, who is cleaning the dining room."

"Oh." Holly sniffed and wiped her eyes. "I'm sorry..." She shook her head. "It was so rude of me not to say goodbye."

"Don't worry, Maggie and I had it all under control." Cassie reached out and gave Holly's arm a squeeze. "I know this is the dumbest question, but are you okay? Do you need me to stay over again tonight?"

"I think I've kept you away from your family for long enough," Holly said with a watery smile and hugged Cassie. A small yelp made her remember she had Harry in her arms. "Oh, shoot, I'm sorry, Cassie. I think I got a bit of dog hair on your dress."

"Don't worry about it. I can assure you I've had a lot worse than a few dog hairs on my clothes," Cassie rolled her eyes.

"Yes, I remember." Holly managed a smile as she remembered a few times Cassie had come to her house with baby food stains on her clothes or needing help cutting a sweet out of her hair. "Our boy was rather messy, wasn't he?"

"That he was." Cassie's eyes lit up as they spoke about her now fifteen-year-old son, Zak.

"How is he holding up through this?" Holly realized she'd been so deep in her own grief about losing her husband of twenty-eight years she'd forgotten everyone else had lost him too.

"He was devastated. You know how much Zak adored Chris," Cassie told her.

"Chris adored Zak too," Holly sucked in a shaky breath. "They were so close."

As if on cue, Zak appeared, "Hey, Aunt Holly, I've put all the spare chairs and fold-out tables back in the basement."

"Thank you, Zak," Holly looked at Cassie's son. At fifteen, Zak was the spitting image of his father, but had his mother's thick golden-brown hair that Holly and Maggie had always envied. Zak was also as tall as his father, Seth Kendrick, who was six-foot-two. "Did you take one of the fridge tarts I told you to take?"

"Thank you, Aunt Holly, I did." Zak walked up to her and hugged her before turning to his mother. "Mom, dad's ready to leave if you are." He looked at Holly again. "I'm sorry, Aunt Holly, but I have a paper due for school that I need to finish."

"I completely understand," Holly assured him. "You've been such a great help today." She looked at Cassie. "You all have."

Holly reached out and gave Cassie's hand a squeeze.

"I have our coats," Seth Kendrick, Cassie's husband, came up behind them.

Holly noticed that Cassie instantly stiffened when Seth arrived. When he reached out to help Cassie with her coat, she snatched it away from him and held it over her arm. Holly saw

Seth's eyes darken, but he looked away before she could see the emotion in them.

"Here, Zak." Seth plastered a smile on his face as he gave his son his coat.

Zak took his coat, and hugged and kissed Holly, "I'll come help finish the boxes tomorrow," he promised.

Zak was helping her box up Chris' stuff. Her eyes immediately misted over at the reminder that they were packing her husband's life away bit by bit. She pulled Zak tight and closed her eyes. Zak was never just Cassie and Seth's child. The moment Cassie had announced she was pregnant with him, he had become hers and their other life-long best friend, Maggie Bridger's, child as well. They had been there through all the 'Zak moments' with Cassie and Seth. He had been the balm that soothed her and Chris' souls when they realized they would never have kids.

Cassie, Seth, and Zak lived two blocks away, but Zak would cycle to their house every second Saturday morning in the summer to go fishing with Chris. While growing up, Holly and Chris were his babysitters. They had never missed a birthday, not even this year. Chris had been sick, but he had refused to miss out on Zak's special day. Knowing Chris was so ill, Zak had decided to have his birthday at Holly and Chris' house with just his family. He was the world's most special kid and had brought so much joy to their lives.

"Thank you, honey." Holly reached out and gave his upper arm a gentle squeeze. "But there is no hurry."

"I promised Uncle Chris," Zak's beautiful blue eyes misted over. "I'm not going to let him down."

"I know," Holly's voice grew hoarse as she let him go. "But

he will understand that you also have school projects to do."
She gave him a kiss on the cheek.

"Can I go put Harry in his bed?" Zak asked.

Holly nodded and handed over the exhausted puppy, who
had been spoiled by the influx of people into the house. Zak
took Harry, who opened his eyes and yawned as Zak took him
to his bed.

"If you need anything…" Seth told her, reaching over to give
her a hug and kiss.

Holly looked into his eyes. She could see the pain there, but
she was sure there was a lot more to it than the pain of losing
Chris, who had become one of Seth's best friends.

"Thank you, Seth." Holly forced a smile. She didn't know
how much longer she could hold on before she dissolved into
another emotional puddle of heartache and tears.

Seth's Adam's apple bobbed as she saw him fighting down
the tears. Maggie had always joked that she never married
because Holly and Cassie had gotten the last two perfect men
left. Holly had often thought about that statement when they'd
gotten together for a function or social gathering. Holly had to
breathe in as images of Chris' laughing face flashed through her
mind as he played a game of football with Seth, Zak, Holly,
Cassie, and Maggie.

"Harry is in bed," Zak called, coming down the stairs and
saving Holly from collapsing to her knees as the pain once again
engulfed her.

"I guess that's us," Cassie said with a tight smile as she
smartly dogged Seth's arm, going around him to step up to
Holly for a hug. "Are you sure you don't want me to stay?"

When Cassie pulled away from Holly, she saw the desperation in Cassie's eyes and frowned. She wanted to ask Cassie if she was okay, but for some reason, Holly felt she couldn't in front of Zak or Seth. So Holly once again gave her friend a forced smile.

"Okay, well, call me if you need anything," Cassie made Holly promise before saying goodbye and leaving. "I'll check in tomorrow."

Holly stood staring out her front door, watching Cassie put her arm around her son as they walked to the car while Seth kept his distance. She cocked her head to the side and frowned, wondering what was happening with Seth and Cassie. While Holly had been involved in her own emotional hell for the past year, she hadn't missed the subtle hints that something was wrong between them.

Holly watched the doors close and the car drive away until the lights faded into the distance. It reminded her how her life before today had disappeared into her distant past. She closed her eyes and swallowed as she sank to the floor. Holly didn't care about her nosey neighbors, silk stockings, or crazily expensive dress and shoes which Maggie had insisted she bought for today. She could no longer hold back the flood of tears and excruciating pain that had been boiling inside her for the past two weeks.

Two weeks of watching the one person in this world she loved more than life itself take his last breath. Watching and feeling completely hopeless to do anything to stop it. How did you fight death? It had slowly pulled Chris towards it over the past ten months. Ten years ago, they had gone to war in a battle against cancer, and they had won. What a glorious day that had been when Chris had held up the scans that showed he was clear. There was hope, treatments, and a promising outcome during that fight. All things to keep them positive, pushing forward, and not giving up the fight.

But ten months ago, Chris had collapsed, and the doctors had given him two years maximum. No, hope, no treatments, or promising outcomes. There was only pain management, a diet change, and a care plan this time. This time, when Holly and Chris had seen Chris' scans, they clasped hands so tightly she could feel his fear and the resounding ache in his heart. Their eyes mirrored their shock and confusion. At that moment, there was still the burning hope that if he would beat it once he could do it again. There must be a way.

But one by one, the doctors, holistic healers, and every other snake oil cure they could find slowly shut down their hope. While she refused to give up, Holly could feel Chris slowly slipping away as he accepted his fate. No matter how much Holly tried to get him to stay and fight, she could feel their future's expiry date was closing in on them. They were no longer fighting. They were getting ready to say goodbye as they tried to make the most of each day. Chris did his best to mask the pain when he could and refused to spend his last days bedridden. Holly had refused to just let him be cared for by a nurse sent to them to help her. She had made the nurses teach her all they could about caring for him and helping him.

Holly had refused to let him go to a care facility and instead had set up their home so he could be in the place they had built together. The place they had called their home since the third year of marriage twenty-eight years ago today — ten days before Christmas. Ten used to be Holly's favorite number, and now she knew she shouldn't, but she hated it because ten years was all they were given after Chris' last fight with cancer. Ten months was all he was given out of the two years the doctors had told her they had. Ten months of no more planning for Christmas, birthdays, or anniversaries. Ten months of waking up and signing in relief to know Chris was still alive, only to hold her breath once again, hoping he'd make it through the day. Waking every few minutes to check he was still breathing.

Ten months of getting angry at the universe for the injustice of making such a good soul suffer like she watched him do each day. Ten months of trying to understand what the point of it all was. Ten months of trying to put on a brave face and make promises to the man she loved that she had no idea if she would be able to keep them. Ten months of feeling guilty each time she mentioned tomorrow because there was no guarantee he had one. Ten months of walking the thin line of wanting him to let go so he could be at peace and not in pain while the other part of her wanted him to hold on with everything he had because she selfishly didn't want him to leave her. She still needed him because he was her everything; without him, every breath she took was painful.

Holly leaned back against her open front door and pulled her knees up to her chin as the tears flooded her cheeks and drenched the skirt of her dress. She rocked as the sobs racked her body. Holly let the flood of pain crash over her in a tumble of emotion. Holly didn't know how long she'd sat there for when Maggie, who had been cleaning the house, found her.

"Holly!" Maggie breathed and ran towards her friend, dropping to her knees and pulling Holly to her. "Oh, honey."

Maggie held Holly, wrapped her arms around her friend, pulled her close, and let the pain pour out of her as her tears streamed down both of their cheeks.

"How am I supposed to go on, Mags?" Holly pressed her head into Maggie's shoulder. "I can't sleep in our room because it's too empty and cold. The memories haunt me and torment me of a time when we were happy. When we would choose what we would watch that night, plan the next day, the next week, or Christmas vacation."

"I know, honey," Maggie sniffed. "I know it's hard right now, and I wish I had some magic words that would take it all away and make it right. But what I can tell you is that you're not alone. I'm always here for you, and it will be okay. Maybe not today or tomorrow, but it will be, and you just have to push through until that day."

"The stars may still come out each night, the sun may rise each day, and the earth may still turn," Holly sobbed. "But nothing in my world will ever be the same again. How could it be when I lost the biggest and best part of me?"

Go to www.amazon.com/dp/B0C1F4SVBS to get your copy!

VIP READERS

Subscribe Here!

Don't miss the
Giveaways, competitions,
and 'off the press' news!

Don't want to miss out on my giveaways, competitions and 'off
the press' news?
Subscribe to my email list.
It is FREE!
Go to https://dl.bookfunnel.com/daorxdf4jo

BAR HARBOR

Go to https://dl.bookfunnel.com/daorxdf4jo for my free book which starts the Secrets in Maine Series and catch up with my other bestselling books.

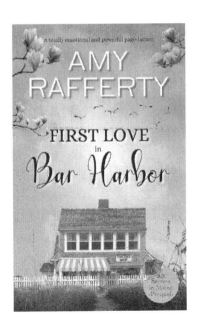

Her life is picture-perfect...until one day she discovers the truth

Grab your tissues and go on a journey to **Bar Harbor**, by Amy Rafferty, "The Queen Of Gorgeous Clean Mystery Romance". Start a heartwarming mystery family saga set in a charming beach resort town in New England.

Love is in the air in Bar Harbor ... but will it wash away with the tide?

For many years, Logan Hall was just an off-limits crush. Her brother's best friend. But when his parents task her with planning Logan's farewell party, Hope Wright finally edges her way into his life. Hope is quickly swept up in a whirlwind summer romance as she works alongside Logan. They spend 10 glorious days together. And then everything comes crashing down.

Logan's ex—teen superstar Melissa Shaw—comes to the party, and his parents make it clear the two are getting back together.

When the phrase 'daughter-in-law' is tossed around in reference to Melissa, Hope decides she must leave. She boards an early plane to Boston, where she attends college.

Nine months later, Hope returns to Bar Harbor, but nothing will ever be the same.

Discover "First Love In Bar Harbor," the prequel in Amy Rafferty's Secrets In Maine Series, and embark on a heartwarming journey of love, forgiveness, and strong family bonds.

For the best experience, read the books in order and enjoy the ride!

MORE BOOKS BY AMY RAFFERTY

Do you love my sweet wholesome romance stories? If you haven't read my other books catch up with them all below.

Please head to my website to check out my books and lots of my other freebies and news!
https://www.amyraffertyauthor.com/

ABOUT THE AUTHOR

Hi wonderful people,

Having been described as 'The Queen of Gorgeous Clean Mystery Romance' I am delighted that you are here. I write sweet women's romance fiction for ages 20 and upwards. I bring you heartwarming, page-turning fiction featuring unforgettable families and friends, and the ups and downs they face.

My mission is to bring you beach reads and feel-good fiction that fills your heart with emotion and love. You will find comfort in my strong female lead role models along with the men who love them. Fill your hearts with family saga, the power of friendship, second chances and later-in-life romance. I write books you cannot put down, bringing sunshine to your days and nights.

Thank you for being here and reading my books x

FOLLOW ME ON MY SOCIALS HERE:

Not only can you check out the latest news and deals there, you can also get an email alert each time I release my next book.
Follow me on Bookbub
https://www.bookbub.com/profile/amy-rafferty

I always love to hear from you and get your feedback. Email me at-
books@amyraffertyauthor.com

Follow on Amazon-
Amy Rafferty
https://amazon.com/author/amyrafferty

Sign up for my newsletter and get a free gift,
HERE!
https://dl.bookfunnel.com/et26h8ozl3

Join my 'Amy's Friends' group on Facebook

HERE!

https://www.facebook.com/groups/1257329798446888/